To

MW01138951

Thank You

Raymond Schmidt

14 Oct 17

Nicholas and Veronica

A Love Story

RAYMOND G. SCHMIDT II

Archway Publishing
1663 Liberty Drive
Bloomington, IN 47403
www.archwaypublishing.com
1 (888) 242-5904

ISBN: 978-1-4808-5222-8 (sc)
ISBN: 978-1-4808-5223-5 (e)

Library of Congress Control Number: 2017954768

Print information available on the last page.

Archway Publishing rev. date: 09/18/2017

Contents

Prelude

In a parallel universe many eons ago a creature found itself in existence. It didn't know where it was; as a matter of fact it didn't have the definition of the concept of where, or what it could refer to as a point of reference. It only knew that it was cognoscente of its being and self-protection became the primary issue. This entity could observe the existence of other things both material and energy that existed and as such determined to find out if it could discern its makeup and origin. *"To begin with"* it reasoned, *"If I am to continue my existence, which is paramount, I must develop a language and set out an orderly structure so I know what I have learned and how to improve on it."* Since the creature had no way of knowing what it was to do next, as it had no point of reference, or how to attempt to establish control over other things that existed it determined that surely language was of the most importance. With that it determined to establish a line of systematic processes that could be retained for reference.

This particular story centers on the formation of what became known as the Christian world.

"The first thing to do is to form an intelligent manner by which I can determine what is and what I only perceive it to be. So the first word in my new language will be the context of my existence and I shall refer to myself as I." Since I had no way of drawing from past experiences it determined that it was the first of its kind and although it didn't know why, it knew it existed for a purpose. "Purpose; now there's a word that should be recorded." Yet I have nothing to record it on so I shall develop a structure whereby I can keep a permanent record and I'll call it a book."

In the process of things as I developed the language and recorded it in the book I determined that the word "it" would not completely identify and justify his presence. It knew that a more dignified and all-encompassing word would be needed to explain its' existence. After much contemplation the entity finally decided that it would record itself as God. "God, now there is a dignified identity for I." So he recorded his new name with the first smile as it was pleasing to him. He recorded the pleasant feeling and assigned the word to that feeling as a smile. The language was coming rapidly now as God decided that all things would be created with structure and for a purpose. Since god was making up things as it went along he decided that the thing that he had created as a living creature should identify itself as something other than "that entity" that he was referring to so he selected the word man. When recording, god would refer as an identity of his creation in the concept of he or him. This set into motion a chain of events that opened new worlds and understanding. God determined that although he could gather and separate energy and matter to suit his purpose he was disposed to create a replica of himself and identify it as a human.

Man was now his entity and god was his name yet he felt incomplete as he had no way to foster a relationship as no one else existed. He then determined to create another creature as a help mate to the human. He was aware that if he was going to continue to exist and if his existence was to have meaning his creation would have to be such so that the human and his help mate would be able to recreate other living cognoscente creatures to continue and insure his existence. God determined that everything that existed came from him yet he could not explain where he came from. With that in mind he determined that the issue of his existence would be put aside for another time. So in order to protect his souvenir state and still continue his progression of perpetuating himself he resolved that all other entities, humans, would be formed in a parallel universe. The logic was that if his creations knew of him but couldn't get to him he would not be subject to any unintended consequences. Since he determined that the humans would exist in a parallel universe and he wanted a closer contact he would create yet another universe that he called heaven and he created immortal beings that he called angels. Angels, he determined, would be immortal and serve him forever without question. The idea seemed sound yet if a mistake was made in the creation of the angels it was that he gave them free will. Since all angels are not equal and all angels were immortal he determined that even though it was a chance, it was a chance that he was willing to take. As it turns out one of his brightest and intelligent angels also had been created with cunning and deceit as a principle feature in his DNA. Eventually this angel, Lucifer decided that he could take over and oust god as the leader. Of course this attempt failed and Lucifer and his followers were expelled from the heavens. God was not of a mind to create another universe at the time so he decided to send them to the universe where the humans lived.

He wanted his humans to be aware of their existence and of his so he taught them the meaning of words and how to record them. After a time, satisfied that he was indeed making progress to a guaranteed continuation of himself he determined that his human in the form of man with his helpmate would reproduce and populate this new universe.

It soon became apparent that man and his helpmate that he called woman, although they were substantially of his own being, had a tendency to wander off the path that he had established for them. He observed this phenomenon for a time and determined that his creation was somewhat different than he. Not only were they different but they were influenced by Lucifer and his followers. The humans would develop into amazing creatures and in so doing formulated ideas of their own. So god determined that he would establish a time frame by which each of the creatures he had created, not including the angels, would have the opportunity to become aware of his existence, pass on through knowledge and records of the recreation of itself and eventually die. After all a series of immortal beings like those that he had created for the heavens would someday come into conflict with his being and might determine to take it away from him. He, of course was not going to put up with that again. Remembering that self-preservation was paramount he made man and woman in a fashion that they would wear our after a period of time.

What he found was that man had a tendency to put together material things that they did not understand and proclaim those things to be gods. God was aware of the influence that Lucifer and his demons had on the humans but elected to leave things as they were. As the population grew they clustered into groups of like-minded humans, a word he determined would be right for man, and found strength in their unity. While this was good for the perpetuation of mankind it caused problems in and of itself. Each group would form a cohesive society for the purpose of self-protection and had the tendency to want to control the others. This prompted god to record what we now call unintended consequences. While this proved to be good for the expansion of the human race it caused conflicts that could only be resolved from within the assigned universe and at times left no room for god.

One way the humans would seek to differentiate themselves was to select different gods to serve their purpose and exalt them above all the other gods known to man. Man, while he collectively formulated a structure of civilization also had a tendency to be self-centered, selfish and self-indulgent. At first god thought that perhaps he had made a mistake in attempting to establish controls over these humans but eventually he determined that rather than a mistake it was a blessing in disguise. "Blessing: now there's a word that I can use for my creation. I will bestow favor on those who follow my word and call it blessings. On the other hand for those who decide not to abide by my wishes, reason dictates that I establish something that will make them aware of the facts that they are not following my commands. These I shall call punishments."

At this point he determined that whatever he wished was in fact a command to be followed.

As he watched his creation develop he noticed that the

older ones who called themselves parents would enact a punishment on the younger ones called children and for a time it would serve to keep them in line. On the other hand he observed that as the child grew and became an adult they would have a tendency to go off on their own way. His conclusion was that the punishment he evoked to keep them in line had to be one so horrendous that it would gain the attention of the humans and they would always want to follow God to get the blessings. One of the problems that god ran into though was the fact that when he created man he not only made them in his own image he also gave them a free will. Free will is essential to the establishment of this group yet the very thing that dictates free will also carry with it the possibility that free-will gets in the way of obedience and receiving blessings. Another one of those unintended consequences was the presence of Lucifer. As previously listed Lucifer was a deceiver and found the humans very gullible and it was easy to get them to follow his lead.

Man in his finite wisdom first came to the conclusion that he was there to serve god and due to his knowledge being limited to self he eventually concluded that god was meant to serve him. Since man couldn't see god they established material things to represent their gods as they saw them. One such sect formed the gods of the zodiac according to western standards. Unknown to the man others around the universe existed and each in their own time using the stars as their guide formed their own gods and entities to follow.

God was intrigued with the thoughts of his humans to create other gods that would serve their purpose so he decided to create yet another parallel universe where he would place these gods that the humans concocted to see where this might lead. One sector of the humans created a dozen gods out of the signs of the stars and called them the gods of the zodiac. These gods would, from time to time filter into the universe where the humans existed and influence them and their way of thinking. Since there were twelve of them god decided that he would separate them into four groups of three and place each group in one of the four corners of that universe. The first group of three he decided would be inhabited by Capricorn who feared to fail; Libra who feared making decisions and Taurus who feared change. How they came to be is of little importance for the purposes of this record but one day the fact that it was even recorded at all will play a significant role in the development of civilization. The human was intertwined into this fabric and fostered the as a byproduct of this creation or the advancement of life as we know it today could not have existed without it.

Taurus the bull loves a great argument and will fight for whatever he wants. He is extremely annoying sometimes but only because he wants your attention. Extremely an extrovert he enjoys being a super hero (the one to come to the rescue), and he is very self-centered and will always do what it takes to get absolutely his very own way. He's a lover of sleep and not easily motivated. Of all of the zodiac signs he considers himself absolutely the most attractive. He can be kind when it suits his purpose. He didn't want anything to change and he simply wanted things to stay as they were for all eternity. After all he was self-indulged. *Besides* he rationalized *I don't know what would happen if I changed things.* This lasted only for a short while. Short in terms of the cosmos and so he got restless. Taurus is accompanied by Capricorn who feared to fail and Libra who feared making decisions. Their time and place is in another universe so only sporadic reverences will be made throughout time in the human universe.

God wanted to insure that man had a way to eventually join him in eternity and celebrate his blessings so he formed the idea of sending his son to show the way. The idea that god had a son became excepted by this new Christian group and in this manner they decided that even though they could not know the ways of god as he had determined it to be, and since he was the one to proclaim that he indeed has a son many picked up on the idea and resolved to follow god no matter what while others determined that in spite of the evidence they would reject his blessings and grace. The Christians determined that they are indeed only partially able to grasp certain concepts of god so they established as part of their beliefs that they could not know the ways of god as such they would simply accept them as truths.

One method that he took to insure that the story of his son's birth was remembered was to perpetuate an everlasting idea that each and every year the event would be remembered and celebrated. One method he used was that of insuring a human was born with the intent of spreading the good news to the young. Since children like toys that grab their attention this individual would create those types of things that could be related to and show a relationship with God. He knew that a simple human, no matter how intent he was at spreading the good news would eventually die and his work with him. Giving this as a premises God allowed one individual to live a long time, much longer than normal, and favored him with the gift of spreading joy through making and giving toys.

One such individual was born at the beginning of what we here on earth call the fifth century. This individual was named Nicholas.

Chapter 1

Nicholas lived about fifteen hundred years ago, in the year of our Lord 402 AD. He was born the thirteenth child of seventeen, close to the small village of Oy-Land. His family were timbermen, log cutters who supplied the needed trees to the merchants of Oy-Land. As it turned out, Nick was the youngest son, and in accordance with family tradition, it was his responsibility to foster the family's good name. Somewhat like many communities as they developed, the oldest son inherited the responsibility of carrying on the family name and inheriting the estate when the time came. It differed in respect to the responsibilities of directing the financial affairs of the family, so that was passed on to Nick. He always took this responsibility seriously; even as a young child, he realized his duties and took special care to dedicate himself to learning how to maintain the books.

As it turned out, he was a frail individual and would have never lasted in the rough country. He did some short excursions with his father and brothers but always returned to the books that he was especially adapted to. His four younger sisters would tease him, as they were physically stronger and always managed to put him down in any physical confrontation. Physically, he never reached five foot four inches, and it wasn't until much later in life that he managed to put on any respectable amount of weight. Most of the time, his family and those who met him just called him the runt. At first, he resented it and delved deeper into his books and shied away from social affairs.

Once while attending the weekly service, he heard the story of Zacchaeus, who was small in stature but was specifically called by Jesus to come down out of his ivory tower and was ordered to prepare to meet him in his home for lunch. Keeping that in mind, Nick determined that physical stature wasn't nearly as important as attitude.

He resolved to alter his outlook on life and present himself to the others for who he was, not how he looked. With this new resolution, he resolved to move out of his parents' home and took up residence in a new home that he had constructed. Since he was a successful accountant and able to take care of the financial responsibilities of his immediate family, other people soon became aware of his special abilities. They would hire him to keep track of their business interests. Since the town of Oy-Land housed several wealthy merchants, his fame spread, and soon he had all the business he could handle.

He started by hiring a student named Korinthos and teaching her the ways of the business. It was a strange relationship, as no one had ever heard of hiring a girl to do this type of work. He met with a lot of resentment, as women were not considered capable of such tasks. Even the local pastor expressed his doubts about spending so much time alone with a female, even though it was during the day on the busiest street in town.

Nick just shrugged off their concerns and replied that

he had selected her based on her abilities as a book-keeper, despite her being a woman. For a short period of time, his business suffered, as the community was sure that he had taken leave of his senses. Those few who stuck with him prospered, as a lot of the reforms they accomplished to enhance their businesses reflected substantially larger dividends than those who had stopped using his services due to the difference of opinion. When the annual business banquet was held, his clients were continuously the recipients of the awards for most successful and innovative establishments for three consecutive years.

Two merchants received the most coveted awards of "most successful" and "most innovative" for the year. Mr. Woodword, the table and chair merchant whose merchandise had become famous for many miles around, stood up to receive his award as the most innovative. As he did so, he shocked the entire town by announcing he had courted and asked for Korinthos' hand in marriage. Korinthos, of course, was Nick's assistant, and although she had accepted and he was going to miss her, he wasn't sorry because her younger sister, Elizabeth, had been working as an understudy for the past year. Of course everyone clapped and congratulated Mr. Woodword for his good fortune, as he now was to have the brightest young woman in town to attend to his business.

When it became Mr. Oak's turn to accept his award for financial success, he also announced that he had been toying with the idea of expanding and with the suggestion of Elizabeth, he had contacted some of the merchants on the wharf and had made arrangements to spread his business along the coastline. Elizabeth was to travel to the other coastal towns, chaperoned of course, and make inquiries into the possibility of expanding his business. As it turned out, she was not only an idealist but also a successful salesperson. In spite of the many rejections, mainly because she was a woman, she proved tenacious in her endeavors, and when she returned, she brought back several small orders and one that was so large that he had to hire two extra skilled plainsmen to fill it.

With that as a success, he asked her to take complete charge of his new shipping department and was pleased to announce that she had agreed to work for him, yet under the name of Nicholas' business. He was happy to be able to engage her services but was disappointed that he had not been able to steal her away from Nick.

Within less than seven years, Nick's financial advising and bookkeeping business expanded, and now he had seven people on his staff. His latest journeyman was a man named Zakias (Zacchaeus), the same name as the man he had decided to follow and the catalyst in launching his business. He became very fond of Zakias and spent many hours teaching him the proper manner in which to conduct his business. They worked together for four years, and one day, Nick started noting fractures in the reports as he examined them. When he investigated the anomalies, he found many areas that were not in compliance with good financial business practices, so he resolved to investigate the issues further. Korinthos was still with him, although she had married and now had four children of her own.

He had fully expected to lose her when she finally accepted the hand of Mr. Timberwolves, but she had requested to stay on as a part-time employee and consultant.

As she was a trusted, valuable employee, he agreed to the arrangement, and it worked out well for both of them. Mr. Timberwolves had suffered an accident and was temporarily incapacitated for several months, so he agreed to have her continue to work part-time to supplement the family income.

Korinthos went over the transactions for the past year and discovered several areas where Zakias had either inadvertently or on purpose made several glaring errors. Nick had entrusted Zakias with many major accounts, as he knew that he was fully capable of meeting the task. The errors had cost both the merchants and Nick a substantial amount of money. When he approached Zakias about it, Zakias became very defensive and shouted that he was being accused of thievery and wouldn't stand for it. He quit his job and abruptly left town.

Nick, of course, was truly discouraged that his clients had been cheated and made arrangements to return their money. Most of them weren't even aware that they had suffered a substantial loss at Zakias' hands and were truly amazed that Nick would make arrangements for their reimbursement. Although that very action placed him in a financially embarrassing situation, he felt that maintaining his and his family's honor was more important than the financial cost. It took several months to regain his financial footing, and as the news spread, at first he lost several prominent customers. He did not allow himself to be devastated or discouraged though, and after a rocky year eventually started back on the path of success.

One day he was approached by a merchant from the town of Points-Ville. He had originally heard of Nick and his business form a traveler by the name of Zakias who claimed to be his understudy and a representative of Nick's firm. He had weaseled his way into the man's business and managed to swindle him out of a small fortune. He decided to investigate Nick's business and upon making inquiries he discovered that although Zakias had told a partial truth that he actually had left this community under a cloud of suspicion.

He returned, located Zakias and had him detained. He was convicted of his thievery and was now serving a long sentence for his crimes. Nick was very distressed over this yet he determined to reimburse the merchant for his loss. The man at first refused as he stated that he did not hold Nick responsible for the thievery of the other. He only wanted to address the issue to him to ease his mind that the scoundrel had been apprehended and was currently paying the penalty for his misgivings. Nick insisted however, as he stated that since Zakias had been in his employment and he had taught him how to be successful in book keeping so he felt it was his responsibility.

With that as a premise he arranged, although it was very painful, to pay back the money stolen. This action set him back another year and so the world turns. Once again he was visited by a famous man from Points-Ville who had the story relayed to him from the first merchant and was informed that Nick was an honest man. He was so impressed with his honesty that he wanted Nick as his full time financial advisor and book keeper. Of course Nick was exuberant about the offer but when the man insisted that he would have to move to his home town Nick turned the offer down. His stance was that he loved his town and the people and felt a personal attachment to those that he had served for such a long time. The man returned to his home simply not understanding that while financial success is important in life commitment and loyalty were even more beneficial.

As the years passed Nick managed to pull himself out of his financial situation. He eventually started on the path to success for the fourth time in his life and was in the process of having a new house built. Over the years he grew found of helping families in trouble especially those with young children. He had opened a wood toy shop in the back room of his business and made sure to make at least one toy for every child age twelve and under. When they turned eleven he invited them to go to his workshop and build toys for the younger children in their families. This insured that no child was left out as each knew his siblings and what they liked. Nick made it a special point to have each toy marked with his special toy store mark. He actually hadn't had in mind a special marking when he started, it just grew over time. It consisted of the heads of two children side by side and a set of praying hands over their heads. The name of the one who built it for their brothers and sisters rested at the bottom center of the piece. The process worked extremely well and even though he didn't make each piece, he had the satisfaction of knowing everything made was done professionally and he had adults to help when the new kids didn't have the skills to do it right.

One day as he was reflecting on how well things had turned out he asked Elizabeth just how many adults were working in the wood shop.

"Well, let's see," Elizabeth said. "We have twenty-two in the wood shop, eleven in the clothing shop, six in the candle shop, and four full time employees making candy for the kids."

Nick was astounded as he'd not kept track with other things that were going on. "Can we afford all of those people?" he asked.

"No" she replied. "Not if you paid them all, but the majority of their work and the materials are donated and all of the employees enjoy it so much that they always chip in especially around Christmas time."

Nick just shook his head and said, "Isn't the Lord good?"

He found himself and many of his full time employees spending more and more time in the shop. So he decided that to insure that the families weren't left out he had an open offer to all the employees and their families to attend a special meeting on Saturdays and they had an all day picnic. They could enjoy making things for each other or just make it a family day. Many of the people, at first were skeptical about him spending so much time with them but it became a tradition and each year starting in mid-October they would have two months of family employee time. During that time he found that most of the employees and their families were spending more time in the shops than in the office.

This life style had become special and routine all at the same time. Nick really didn't mind it as he found it more and more pleasing as each year passed. He always made sure the customers were taken care of and even invited them to join any time they would like to.

Since his immediate family was lumbermen he was able to obtain a lot of left over scrap wood that in the past had been discarded and he got what he wanted at no cost.

It became his passion and he determined to expand his business to Points-Ville. Since it was a large port town his toy shop became a famous stopping place for travelers and soon his name with his family crest became a symbol of quality.

Once he was established in his new store in Points-Ville he decided to send flyers on the ships to the other ports.

Chapter 2

On one occasion when he just happened to be at the new store taking inventory he met a lady by the name of Veronica. She had seen his ads as the trade ships had come into port and was interested in what this new toy manufacture had to say for himself.

As a noble of the court she spoke with the King and inquired if she could have a leave to pursue this new type of gifts that were advertised. The king initially stated that he had no interest in it but he had a young daughter named Ann who was taken with the pictures and begged her father to let Lady Veronica go. As many young daughters can, she persuaded her father to allow the travel. He drew the line however when Ann suggested that she could accompany the Lady and see these magnificent toys first hand. As any young girl with her father wrapped around her little finger would she kept begging stating that it was very important. None the less when the ship sailed Ann was left on the dock.

The first part of the voyage was without incident and for the first couple of days Lady Veronica wrote in her diary that she was happy because not only was it an opportunity to see the rest of the world, but also got her away from that stuffy castle. "Dear diary." She started it that way for so long that she didn't even think that there was an alternative way to start. Then she thought about it for a moment and decided "Dear diary." Just wasn't enough to express her emotions. "Dearest diary?" "No, that's silly." She related to herself. I need something to bring out the real me." So she settled on "Another exciting day in the life of Veronica." At least for the time being. Having settled that she started to record.

She liked her life well enough but always wondered what was on the other side of the ocean. While she had traveled to France in her younger years it was an official trip and everything was very formal. There was some talk of her betrothal but as a seven year old she had no interest in that. It was for adults and she'd cross that bridge when it happened. Now as a young woman and being from a country that is constantly changing its views on marriage it seemed to be left to her to decide to whom she would marry. Since she was not interested in looking for a suitor at this time she placed those thoughts far back in the reaches of her mind. There was one young man that she had taken a shine to but he was from a far off country and their brief relationship lasted only as long as he was a guest of the King. He left when their job was completed and never met again.

Anyway Veronica was content to leave that for another day as she watched the sun dip below the horizon. That night she woke to the sounds of clinging bells and orders being shouted above the roaring winds. The ship was being tossed about like a cork in a lake disturbed by boulders dropping from the sky. She had not taken the precautions to secure much of her belongings as she had so gingerly laid them out for the next day. For the most part of the night she just clung to the sides of the bed rails and prayed that this wouldn't be her last night on earth. After a rough night she finally managed to get dressed and decided to see if she could determine just what had happened.

As she reached the deck she noticed that all was calm. The sailors were jousting and jibbing at the inexperienced for their obvious lack of ability at meeting the challenge. One of the older seaman in a deep gruffly voice proclaimed that last night was practice for beginner apprentices. He proclaimed that he as a youth had gone through much worse and had even been capsized twice when a forty foot wall of water had overturned his vessel and many lives were lost. According to his story he drifted for eleven days on the open sea and was finally rescued by a small fishing boat off the coast of Norway. It took several months to arrange passage back to the mainland as the winter had set in and when the sea froze over nothing was able to move.

According to his story, while he was marooned in that god forsaken place he had traveled with a small band of gypsies to some of the neighboring towns. Once he had even landed at a place called Points-Ville and had observed that a great amount of trade that occurred there. He claimed that it rivaled the great ports of the crown and he had fallen under the spell of the excitement. Having determined that this was a good place to conduct business he decided that he'd make this a permanent transitional spot and had been coming back every year for the past twenty some odd years.

Lady Veronica initially eyed the old sailor with skepticism as she stacked him physically up against others of his kind. After a short while she became so enthralled with his story that she determined his outward appearance meant little in determining his character. When she mentally compared his stature to that of her ideal sailor she couldn't determine if he fit the bill or if she was being too critical of her expectations. He stood well above six foot and had a deep gash across the forehead. His clothing was unique in that although well worn, displayed a neat and tidy presentation. Without addressing the situation as a direct cognitive thought she determined that she would seek his council and offered him a position on her staff.

He in turn replied that while he would do all in his power to see to it that she was well tended to that he could not accept her offer as he had determined his place in life and was well satisfied with it. She took his council into advice and continued to press him for additional details. Finally he replied, "My Lady, each of us have our own destiny to fulfill and while I am appreciative of the opportunities that you may avail me, I must remain who I am and do what I do best."

Lady Veronica gained a lot of respect for the old sailor and resolved to do her best to insure that he was always looked after, even if he didn't know about it. She instructed her entourage to watch for opportunities to assist him whenever possible but never to make it known that she was the benefactor.

As it turned out the old sailor was an entrepreneur and who through no fault of his own had tried and failed on several occasions to obtain his own ship. As a member of the royal court she had certain persuasions that proved very successful in assisting him in obtaining his own ship.

Once again she took pen to paper and wrote that she

had met the most fascinating man she had ever met and was pleased that she had been able to make his acquaintance. Lady Veronica simply smiled at the fact that she had become so infatuated with him that she had resolved to insure his success no matter what the cost. After all he was just a sailor.

The cost of course was immaterial as with her status in life and the inheritance of more money and land that she could ever hope to count this expense would be only a pittance.

Early the next morning Lady Veronica while standing on the bow made sure that she was in the position to observe and quietly assist whenever the opportunity presented itself. While she was not able yet to get an official status on the man, she knew within her heart that he was a good man and a man of his word. She had several of her people make discrete inquiries about him. As a lady of the court she was in the position to gain information from the captains logs without raising any undue suspicions. She simply told the captain that she was fascinated with how efficiently he maintained everything. With flattery and a few well-placed smiles she got him to offer access to his logs. Veronica found out his name was William of Locksley a resident of the northern part of the great island. He was fiercely independent and although a hard taskmaster always looked kindly to the young inexperienced members of the crew. He was married and reportedly had seven children although she wondered how he had the time to father seven children while always at sea. She supposed that his wife, by the name of Ionad Tapa meaning Stead Fast in Irish was, extremely dedicated to William and as were many women of that time as steady as a rock when it came to bonding with her man.

The more she learned about William the more fascinated she became and even though he wasn't a pleasant looking man she knew he was a man of outstanding character and fiercely devoted to his wife. This deepened her resolve even further to insure he became successful.

At the conclusion of the voyage as Lady Veronica reflected in dramatic fashion in her diary that they had survived several days of bad weather on the sea, her patients were frazzled and she was at the end of her rope. In spite of her excitement and exuberance at the start of the trip she found herself worn and dismayed to be in this small dreary town where the smell of dead fish permeated the air. She thought to herself

"I've been in a lot of unfavorable places in my life, but this one tops them all." " Points-Ville? The jewel of the north sea.?" She was reflecting on Williams definition of the place to set up as a home port. She determined that although it wasn't all it was cracked up to be that she, in her usual manner, would accept life for what it has to offer. So in spite of all of the hardships she was still looking forward to a bright new day tomorrow as the speakers of the weather had stated that tomorrow would be a sunny day.

"I can hardly wait for tomorrow" she told herself. Once again she scribed her feelings. "My clothing will be dry and I will be able to travel away from this God forsaken town into the country. *I'm sure things will be better then."* So she decided that in spite of her current position she was going to make the best of it and enjoy the rest of her day.

After a good breakfast, notwithstanding the smell,

Lady Veronica sent her escort to the stables to see if she could go for a ride in the country. She was surprised when he returned with a rain deer saddled and ready for the ride. As a lady Veronica had never ridden a rain deer before but after a few seconds of consideration said

"Why not? It'll be fun." So she along with eight fully armed battle tested soldiers and the rest of the staff headed off for the forest area. She had been warned that was imperative that she always stay on the trail as the deep woods were filled with critters that would just love to have her over for lunch. As an accomplished rider Veronica dressed for the part and slung a sword at her side with a bow across her back. As an expert in both in training and even engaging in a few battles in her time. The Lady set forth with great confidence. She didn't kid herself though; she was not an accomplished warrior and always made sure she had plenty of back up.

Lady Veronica had arranged for a contingent of three locals to serve as guides and they promised that she would have a joyful day and be back before dark. They started at first light as she had a tough time sleeping and ordered her breakfast before the rooster crowed.

Just as they left the town and crested the first hill she noted that the sun was in deed rising and spreading it's warmth across the land.

"This place is really beautiful," she said. "I can imagine myself in the hills of England just south of London. Rolling hills, a clear light blue canopy, the birds chirping. Why it's almost a carbon copy.

"Yes mam," the boy replied. "During the late spring and early summer the flowers are in full bloom and when it's not raining it's quite a sight."

She smiled at the lad as he was surely full of excitement and was anxious to show off his skills in his ability to identify the scenery in colorful terms. She thought to herself *"This must surely be as new to him as it is to me."* Since she had never ridden a rain deer before she asked, "Is there anything special I should know about the beast."

"Oh, no," the boy replied. "Missy here is gentle as a kitten and always seeks to please her rider. I selected her myself when I was told that you would be riding her. You'll not have to worry yourself about her."

His voice was confident and set her mind at ease so she decided to just sit back and enjoy the ride. This would be a great story to relay when she returned home. Imagine, riding a rain deer.

After they had been on the road for a bit the lad, obviously in charge raised his hand to signal a stop. She edged up close to him and ask what was wrong to which he replied, "Oh, nothing; I just thought you'd like to stretch for a while as even an experienced rider can sometimes become uncomfortable. Besides, look at the valley below with all the yellow and red flowers. I used to come up here with my mother when I was young and we would observe the sites sometimes for an entire day. We won't stay that long today though as I was instructed to be sure to get you back before the sun set. It can get pretty dangerous out here after dark and even your eight soldiers may find it hard to win a battle should it come to that. The marauders have trained wolves and enjoy fleecing the unprotected."

"Don't you think perhaps we shouldn't have come out this far if that's the case?" She replied.

"Oh no," he responded, they would never come out during the day, especially on a beautiful sunny day like this one. She observed a slight smile on his face and concluded that perhaps he was spinning a yarn to add a little excitement to the trip. "Well, its sure comforting to know I have such a competent guide."

After a short stop he indicated that they still had a way to go and he wanted to show her the old castle on the far ridge. "It's a special place in our folk lore as it was the home of a dark and gruesome lord of the land. It's said that he had his subjects chained and dragged over the side of the cliff just to see how many he could kill in one day. Of course that was a long time ago and his decedents have long since gone. All, of course, accept one. You've always have to have one lingering so as to keep the story alive." He chuckled with an undertone that projected a sinister thought. "Well that's an interesting story I can take back with me when I return to my land." She smiled at him.

The ride down the far side was a gentle slope and she thought they made good time. As they reached the valley they were greeted with children laughing and waiving them on. So they were able to stop for a short while at the inn. The guide gave orders to insure the soldiers stayed at the ready in case anyone decided to crash on their party. "Is that really necessary?" She inquired. "No my lady, it's not but it is proper protocol and I don't want anything to go wrong, even on an off chance."

Lady Veronica took it all in stride as she figured that it must be part of the show to impress visitors with a little excitement. As they finished their lunch the young leader approached her and stated that since they had taken so long with this part of the tour that the castle would not be available today or they'd not get back before dark. He extended his hand and stated, "Perhaps another day."

She had been having such a good time that she didn't notice that the clouds had gathered and the sky was being blanketed with overcast. "Are we going to get rained on?" She asked. "No I don't think so" was the reply "but we will have to cut this short and take the short road home. Don't worry though we'll be back long before dark.

Once again they were on the road only this time with haste. The sky's had become darker, the wind was gusting and the limbs of the forest trees were swiping at the caravan on the narrow path. At times the vision was so blurred that it was almost impossible to ascertain the road from an animal path. After they had traveled for about a half hour they rounded a bend to find that trees had been uprooted and an avalanche had blocked the path. The young man in charge called a halt to their travel as he went forward to take stock of the current situation. After a time he returned with grim news. The slide had completely blocked the existing road and the way around was simply too hard to transverse as the rocks were not only slippery but showed no signs of a solid foundation. "I fear that if we continue on this path we'll not be able to make it." The only logical thing left to do was to return to the inn.

Upon approaching the inn they discovered that a horrendous storm had completely devastated the building where they had lunch and it lye in complete rune. They could find no signs of life, even the dogs and cows were missing. "What a strange turn of events." The guide stated as he shook his head. "Well the only place to find shelter before the darkness overtakes us is to go to the castle. At least there we can set up some semblance of defense and regroup for our travel back to town tomorrow." The Lady Veronica, while somewhat concerned elected to look upon this as an adventure rather than a perilous situation.

"Well" she responded "I've been in worse spots with a lot less support." She was referring to her experience once while traveling on the mainland where the French were said to be somewhat between hostile and barbaric. She was much younger at the time and although the experience was harrowing for a young girl only her memory of the actual occurrence lingered as a verboten situation. Now of course she was much more able to take care of herself and as an accomplished marksman and a competent wheeler of a sword had a greater confidence that any adversity could be matched. Besides she had a contingent of eight battle proven soldiers at her side. They gathered everything that they found; some food stuff, some clothing and a few weapons and continued toward the castle.

The wind had died down but the rain was unrelenting and the path was slippery. Finally they made their way to the entrance to the castle to find a few of the people from the inn hovered together trying to assure themselves that everything was going to be okay. As they entered the main area Lady Veronica decided that now was the time to provide real leadership. She gave commands with the authority of a true leader of stature and organized the small shambled group into one area.

Upon receiving a report that one area still existed where the roof was still in tack and was dry she immediately ordered the entire group to proceed to the area and stationed her eight warriors so as to provide a three sixty perimeter. Once accomplished she assigned one of her entourage to make an inventory of what was available and made sure the civilians were all provided with as much clothing and blankets as was available to enable them to reside in as much security as could be accomplished.

The small band from the inn consisted of one old woman with the grit to control her two less organized young maddens, three young boys about seven to nine years of age, two middle aged men both of whom were wounded during the storm and the ensuing battle with a small band of wolves and lastly a very young baby. She couldn't expect much assistance from any of them in an all-out battle but she set them up in such a fashion that they would provide an inner circular protection for the baby in the event it came to that.

They boarded up three of the five entrances to restrict any attempt of an enemy to attack and tightened the circle of defense. That way she could establish a rotation of defense insuring that the guards were always fresh and could be reinforced by the ones at rest if the battle came. Her young guide made a few attempts to provide instructions but soon acquiesced as he was truly amazed at her ability to organize so he simply submitted to her authority. She had wood gathered to make a fire for light and warmth throughout the night and when she was contented that she had done all that she could do to insure survival for the night returned to the fire to get something to eat and obtain warmth. After a while she slowly drifted off to sleep and was hoping to remain that way until her shift came up.

Within an hour the small contingency heard the howling of the wolves and the banging of swords slapped against the shields. Veronica awoke almost immediately and ordered everyone to the ready. They reinforced the three entrances with additional obstacles and opened the traps they had established at the two entrances. She had holes dug three feet deep across the entire entrance way and three feet wide. Then she had some flimsy boards laid across the holes and threw a little dirt over them to insure that before an assailant discovered them he would drop into the hole.

Since she found some spikes exposed on some of the planks she had them lying face up so when the adversary fell into the hole he would have his feet punctured drawing his attention away from the defenders long enough for them to strike a final blow. As the noise grew louder she readied her bow and insured that the safety strap on her sword was unleashed so it would be more readily accessible. One thing that she did at the suggestion from the young guide was to establish several wood piles outside the enclosure and made them ready to set afire as soon as the battle started. This proved to be a God send as they were able to douse the fire in their circle and provide light behind their adversaries. It gave them the advantage of seeing the enemy while the opposition peered into the dark.

At the start of the battle the wolves entered first. With their agility and lack of weight they were easily able to clear the entrance without setting off the traps. Lady Veronica let loose the first arrow which landed squarely in the open mouth of the lead wolf. These were fairly easily dispatched as there were only four of them and the soldiers were trained well. Three barbarians followed in quick pursuit and stepped into the traps. That proved to be an effective deterrent as the three were quickly dispatched. Lady Veronica was able to get off three more shots and was greeted with the howls of at least two of the offenders.

The battle quelled for a short period of time while they apparently were deciding on their next approach.

Lady Veronica noticed that a small spiral stair case led to the next level and determined that their current position was tenuous at best. An all-out attack would render her party helpless to defend against a much larger assault team. Quickly she had the entire civilian population moved up to the next flight and clustered into a corner with no windows.

She asked them to arrange themselves as they had been while in the main room and stated that their main purpose was to protect the young and not get involved in the actual fighting unless it became absolutely necessary.

She positioned the soldiers staggered along the narrow stair well and with bravado in her voice assured them that if they would fight as a single unit and protect each other that they would be able to hold off any force. Once again she positioned several small piles of wood and doused them in a flammable liquid so as to start small fires in the main room and allow the archers the advantage of being able to address their foes.

The second wave of attack started with fortuitous yells and the beating of the swords and spears against the shields. They burst into the main room screaming wildly and stopped only momentarily when they discovered the intended prey was not there. Lady Veronica gave the command and the arrows lit up the piles of wood immediately lighting up the entire room. Then without command the archers started letting the arrows fly. In less than a few seconds the invaders were headed back to the safety of the outside leaving behind at least a dozen of their own. The archers then proceeded to the narrow slits in the wall meant to pursue the adversaries and landed some more devastating blows.

The battle won, the enemy retreated back into the safety of the forest while presumably formulating their next strategy. After a short period of time some of the defenders offered that perhaps they had driven them off and they would not return.

Lady Veronica, while not a full-fledged tactician stated that they would surely come back. After all they would presume that this was an unorganized crew and the first two attempts were just a stroke of luck. She ordered the defensive team to regroup take stock of their equipment available and prepare for another assault.

Only one soldier had been hurt severely and would be out of commission when it came to hand to hand fighting but he assured her that he could still string a bow. They went back into their passive defensive mode in the hope that it would take some time for the opposition to form a new plan and they could get some rest.

By this time the wind had calmed down and the rain stopped. The full moon came out and afforded the defenders the opportunity to observe any incursions from the trees. Fortunately there was a space of about forty yards of open area once they left the forest and it would give the archers ample opportunity to get off some more arrows too inflict as much mayhem as possible before they arrived.

At the suggestion of her young guide they boarded up the two openings and stacked them with as much old furniture as possible to slow the assault. Once accomplished they had nothing left to do except wait. She ordered that the remaining food be distributed and insisted that the soldiers each eat something. After all she reasoned they would need all the strength they could muster when the time came. Once again she gave the command that the defenders return to their rotation basis and leaned against the far wall. It wasn't long before direness overtook her and she nodded her head.

Once again she could hear the beating of the swords against the shields and knew it was time to once more defend. She gave reassurance to the civilians that they were in a good position to ward off the enemy and placed everyone at the ready. As she peered out the slit while reading her bow she could see the dawn overtaking the shadows and was inspired that perhaps it was a sign of hope. The noise, instead of intensifying seemed to drift off into the darkness of the forest.

"Perhaps" she thought to herself *"Perhaps, we've out-lasted them and they will crawl back into their holes."* Cautiously she gave the command for the entire group to get ready to move back toward the town of Points-Ville.

Yet something at the back of her mind still nagged at her and her hair stood up on the back of her neck. She did not know these people and had no way of drawing on her experiences as a tactician to determine if they had really driven off the adversaries or if it was a trap. She elected to let caution be her guide and consulted with the guide and the senior members of the soldier contingency she had with her. The guide assured her that the enemy had fled and it was now safe to return on the trip. Her senior advisors took the opposite view and offered caution. She decided to go with the seniors as they were battle tested and while the guide seemed to know the territory she wasn't sure how much experience he actually had in de-termining the potential risk.

As fortune would have it she had as part of her contingency two of the soldiers who had several years as scout's and they assured her that if the enemy were still out there they would locate them. Perhaps with that knowledge they could assemble a plan on how to skirt them and start their journey back to the town.

With a simple nod of the head she sent them out to see what they could find. In the mean time she attended to anyone who was sick or wounded. Everyone was anxious to resume their path back to safety. The one soldier who had received the injury was confident that he could hold his own and declared that he had only minor scratches. Spirits were high and all were sure they were going to be okay. In just a short while the scouts returned and reported that the enemy had indeed laid a trap along the main road hoping that they, thinking that all was well would resume their travel. The guide and his partner offered that they knew of another route. It would be longer but a lot safer than attempting to deal with the cutthroats in the open. So the decision was made and the small group headed out for the alternate path.

It wasn't long before the scouts reported back that they had encountered a caravan consisting of at least twenty wagons and a large contingent of guards.

They had approached them and were received with joyous repor when they explained what they had been up against and how the Lady Veronica had formulated them into an assembled fighting force. The leader of the caravan offered that he wanted to meet the lady that had defeated the scoundrels at their own game. As it happened they were heading for Points-Ville and would provide the escort necessary to insure her safe return.

Chapter 3

Lady Veronica was thrilled to hear that she was finally out of danger. Although later as she recounted the adventure she still had the thrill of knowing that she had met the enemy on his own terms and managed to overcome the obstacles. Her renditions of this event were held is strictest confidence by all as she charged none to relay the content of the event. She was concerned that the story would filter back to the king and he would in turn clamp down on her ability to travel. So with the exception of her diary it was not recorded in the annuals of her life until a much later date.

Since the caravan moved at a much slower pace than her party originally had, they wound up at the castle again later that day. This time however they had adequate defenses and the guards were posted. Her personal guards were assigned to look after her welfare as the caravan leader stated that they would have nothing to fear from the outside. This gave Lady Veronica and her escort's ample time to explore the castle. She so wanted to do this as she had absolutely no time on the first visit. Now with the fear of attack gone she felt at ease and wanted to see what this place might have to offer. One of the first spots that she entered was the grand hall. It was one of the largest rooms she had ever encountered. It was circular and stretched at least the length of two jousting fields. She could imagine the celebrations that must have taken place in this place when it was fully occupied. The tables would have been placed in a large portion of the outer part of the room while the dance floor would provide for various entertainments to happen simultaneously. She could only imagine it now as there was no furniture present. Most of it presumably had been hauled off and burned for fire wood during the cold winter days.

Her young guide offered his services as he, as he put it, was thoroughly familiar with the castle and its' history. He took her to the large chambers of the immediate family. The Queens bedroom of course was second in size to the kings and could accommodate at least a dozen ladies in waiting as she prepared herself for her daily rounds. The guide stated that it took no less than three hours to prepare her for her daily routine. Off to one side was a walk in closet that was large enough to hang on display no less than a hundred dresses with matching shoes and other apparel. The story was told that the kitchen staff had to start preparing her breakfast at least four hours before she was to eat and since they never knew what mood she was in they had to prepare at least seven varieties so when she finally placed her order they could have it ready in less than ten minutes. Everything went on good for some time until she discovered that the food that she was not eating for the day was being distributed to the poor. Her immediate response was that no food prepared for a queen should ever be given to the poor as they were not worthy. She demanded that all food not eaten by her for her meals was dumped and burned so no one could touch any food destined for her. As Lady Veronica had always been a champion of the little guy she just thought this to be an awful situation. But she admitted that she had never given thought at to the disposition of the food that was not eaten at the meals in her castle. She vowed to herself that she would look into that matter when she returned home.

She spent the remainder of the day inspecting the lay of the land and its proximity to the town. When she asked where the Caravan had started they informed her that it originated in Oy-Land and the route had been established by a prominent businessman by the name of Nicholas. It seemed that although the route was seldom traveled in the old days due to the raiders that Nicholas had convinced the merchants of Oy-Land that large caravans could be established to enable them to spread their wears over greater territories and this policy had proven financially successful. Since The Lady Veronica had initially started her tour with the hope of obtaining some of the now famous toys that came out of the Oy-Land factory she was absolutely thrilled at the thought of going back with the caravan when it returned so perhaps she could meet Nicholas in person. She thought it would make a marvelous addition to her journal and perhaps she could even get a hand inscribed article to present to her niece. When she spoke to the caravan leader he was rather skeptical as to the wisdom of such a move as it was now late in the summer and with fall coming up soon the passes could be blocked by the early rains and then the vast amount of snow that fell. He told her that some years the snow came early and the passes became impassable for months. If that were to happen she would be stuck for months in the small town with nothing to do. He stated that he wouldn't advise it based on the probable conditions that she would meet. Besides he reminded her she had stated that she was planning on returning to her home next month and a trip of this nature would most likely result in her being delayed.

She considered it for a short while then concluded that perhaps the leader was right and she should adhere to the current plan. The next day they started out again on the road to Points-Ville and for a time she was content to just enjoy her travel. They managed to arrive late that day but her quarters were kept intact and ready for her so she was able to enjoy a great hot bath, spend the evening wining and dining and returned to her sleeping quarters late in the evening. As she spoke to her Ladies in waiting and mentioned how thrilling it would be to be able to go to Oy-Land the very thought of it caught hold and she decided to pursue it further in the morrow.

The next morning she woke early to hear a lot of commotion happening at the dock area. She quickly dressed and inquired about all of the excitement and was informed that her ship that was to pick her up had been attacked by the pirates of the sea. Although they had fended off the intruders the ships Capitan and several of the crew members had been badly wounded and the ship had suffered extensive damage. She inquired about the mate that she had taken a liking to and was informed that although slightly wounded he would recover shortly. She decided to seek out his presence to inquire about his health. While there she mentioned that she had considered taking the overland trip to Oy-Land but tentatively decided against it as the ship was due back and she wanted to be able to go with it on its return journey. "Well my Lady, we won't be making that trip any too soon. By the time the ship is fixed and the sailors back on duty the winter will have set in and we'll not be going anywhere till spring."

With this information she returned to the leader of the caravan and requested that she be allowed to return with them to Oy-Land. At first he stated that he'd have to think on it because of her royalty and he would have to decide just what his responsibilities would be in the event anything went wrong. She persisted and wrote a letter to be held by the local constabulary to be sent back to her king in the event something dreadful went array. With that assurance he agreed to allow her to accompany him and his outfit on the return trip. He summonsed a messenger and dispatched him post haste. The courier was a seasoned traveler and had traversed the land on several occasions. He never took the same route twice and moved swiftly on his horse. Since he'd leave in the early morning before dawn he'd make the entire journey in less than a day. The caravan leader wanted the people of his town to be ready to receive her properly as they received very few visitors and even fewer of the royal realms.

Happy that she was able to establish her position as a newest member of the group she decided to go shopping.

She spent the entire day selecting appropriate attire for the winter in Oy-Land and at the suggestion of the local merchants stocked up on plenty of warm winter clothing and gifts to present to the people of that town. Of course there were many to assist her and by the time she was done with the purchases for the day she had to purchase five additional pack mules. The caravan leader was surprised at the amount of luggage she had loaded and quipped, "My Lady you'll not be there for years." She smiled back and said it would be a long hard winter and she wanted to be prepared. Early the next day they were back on the road again. She had hired six additional members to watch over the gifts as she wanted her entourage to be able to concentrate on their assigned task and not have their attention diverted from their primary responsibilities. One of the soldiers made a special note that he thought that she was the most thoughtful royalty that he had ever encountered and was proud to be in her service.

They stopped at the old castle again for the stay overnight and Lady Veronica was able to investigate further. She determined that she really liked this old place and although it would take some doing it could be restored. Making notes in her diary she jotted "This will be a perfect place for a second summer time home." Actually she filled the better part of three pages listing details, and drawing sketches. The hills would be alive with the pleasant fragrance of the flowers and she even had in mind that it could be reestablished and used as a half way place for the two towns. After giving it some consideration she decided to inquire about the deed to the place. At first no one wanted to speak of it as this place had been haunted both by ghost and the vagabonds who traveled through these woods. Most of the people simply wrote it of as a foolish inquiry but the Lady Veronica was determined to follow through. That evening while they were preparing the sleeping arrangements she asked the caravan leader if he had any knowledge of who might have claim to this territory. At first he just chuckled at the thought that anyone would want to refurbish the old castle as it had long been forgotten and claimed by whoever wanted it at the time. "Surely" she responded "there must be a deed. I can tell by the town that I was recently in that civilization has taken root and somebody must know who the proper owner of this wonderful palace is." Well My Lady we can certainly ask when we arrive at Oy-Land. Come to think of it, I'll bet if anyone knows Nicholas will. He has been the keeper of the books for several years now and if anyone would know, it would be him."

With that information Lada Veronica was content to examine the lay of the land in more detail as she was sure in her own mind that this would make a beautiful summer villa. She had mentioned it to a few of the merchants and they seemed to think that once it was secured they might be interested in setting up a shop there. One lady, an elderly woman stated that she had a cottage not far from there years ago. The roughens had forced her out when they killed her husband and crippled her only son. She described how it was a beautiful place and she always had a variety of flowers growing from early spring to late fall when the snow was deep. Even then she offered, that the edelweiss, a winter snow could be seen on the lea ward side of the mountains most of the winter except of course when it really got bad. When the Lady Veronica asked how often that happened the old lady kind of giggled and replied "Every year dear."

It seems the flower seeds were a favorite of the Germanic tribes who came through. They had a reputation for being Barbarians and were fierce fighters; however in years past they had settled with their families in that region and had planted the flowers as they were a sign of good luck. Over the years the tribes moved on but the flowers continued to grow each year without attention.

The old ladies eyes lit up as she said "You can still see them in some areas where the current Neanderthals as she called them haven't stomped them out." As Lady Veronica turned to leave, the old woman with a tear in her eye asked that if the Lady did actually get a hold of the castle if she could move back into her home. It was the home of her great grandmother and she often regretted having to leave. With a parting gesture the Lady Veronica responded "I'll see what I can do."

She decided to see if she could find the cottage that the old woman was talking about and ask the caravan leader if he had any idea as to where it might be as she really would like to see it. "Well you're in luck" he responded "we'll be passing within a stone's throw when we go through the pass." When she inquired as to the location of any other townships in the area she was informed that there were at least three more small villages within one to two days in the mountainous areas but they were by and large isolated due to the narrow roads, the bandits, and the severe weather most of the year. The wheels started spinning in her mind as she allowed her imagination to take flight. Her mind's eye envisioned making the castle a hub for merchant traffic.

As she talked with her escorts they expressed at how they were impressed at how she had taken charge during the first ensuing battle and how she laid out her plans in detail without the necessity of actually writing it all down. Those with her caught the fever and some were asking that they be included in rebuilding the area. All of the soldiers looked upon the assignment favorable and some even spoke of making a request to be made a permanent part of the guard.

For the next two days they traveled without stopping except to change the guard and stretch the legs. Those not actually on duty spent their off duty shift making themselves as comfortable as possible and catching any sleep that was available. When Lady Veronica asked why they had to continue the movement without rest the leader replied that this was the most dangerous part of the journey and they never stopped while in this valley. The cliffs on both sides were covered with dense forest and marauders would sneak up while they were at rest and attempt to steal and kill the members. He said not to worry though as it was a routine action and the members were used to it. Once they completed the trip through the valley they came out on a vast gentle sloping land that stretched as far as the eye could see. He told her that now that the harrowing part of the journey was over the rest of the way to Oy-Land would be an easy ride.

They traveled at a leisurely pace for the next four days and the Lady Veronica was amazed at the beauty of the area. She had only seen land this pretty as the rolling hills south of London. From her position it looked like the valley stretched forever. The mountains on either side raised to heights well beyond the site of vision and in the early morning gave off a purple glow that gave one the feeling that they were in heaven.

The days were shorter now as it was a sign that the winter would soon arrive. She noticed that the nights seemed to be colder than at Points-Ville but the guide explained that they were several thousand feet above sea level and the air was always colder in this region even though they were in a valley. She really didn't mind the cold though as she had experienced this type of clement when she had visited the area called the Alps Mountains some years back. She knew that she was well cared for and adequately dressed for the occasion.

As they started to set up camp at the end of the fourth day they were met first with what seemed to be an invasion of nomads. At first they seemed to be as numerous as the flowers on the gentle slops and it looked for a while that they would be overtaken. Although the defenders fought valiantly they were vastly outnumbered and it was soon apparent that they would not be able to fend off the invasion. The caravan leader shouted orders to form a circular defense and they as experienced troops followed his commands. At one point he shouted that they had taken him by surprise and to break the spear of their thrust he would have to send a defensive shield to the point to break the spirits of the invaders. As he was preparing for a final thrust they heard a large noise coming from over the hill. "It seems the Calvary has arrived." His voice displayed a sense of excitement and relief.

As it turned out the hordes had been raiding the outlining villages for the past couple of weeks and since they were expecting them to be in the area about this time so they had been keeping an eye out for the barbarians. The leader was greatly relieved and they were able to set up a comfortable camp for the evening. "I've never seen that many congregated in an effort to raid in this area." The leader was telling the Lady Veronica when they were informed that the back of the assault was broken. This one was unexpected at this time of the year and this far north. He had served for several years in the south eastern provinces and had known that they did exist. He couldn't imagine what drove them this far north this time of the year.

The next day was a long trip and everyone was on their guard until they reached the township of Oy-Land. Everyone was happy when the trip was over. Since the messenger had proven once again to be swift and efficient the quarters for the Lady Veronica were all ready and she with her entourage were able to clean up change and enjoy a good evening. She was informed that a celebration was planned for tomorrow and would last well into the evening. The town was happy to have her as she was a celebrity and royalty. The tale of her heroics during the initial battle with the hoards had been repeated and she was held in high esteem.

Chapter 4

The next morning was filled with excitement as she was introduced to the locals. The official mayor of the town, who just happened to be Nicholas, took her around to the merchants on Main Street. In each business she was treated like a queen and offered more fine eats and drinks. Having been exposed to this before she was careful to accept only small bits so she wouldn't wind up full and not be able to conduct herself properly later in the day.

At the end of the tour Nicholas took her to his office and introduced her to his staff. He concluded the tour by taking her to the toy shop in the back of the office. Over the years he had expanded it three times and was planning on another expansion after the winter months. Right now they were gearing up for their winter event.

As it turned out she was quite talented with arts and colors and spent many of her waking hours over the next several weeks working in the shop. Many of the workers were volunteers and the majority of them were actually too young to be employees. When Veronica mentioned it to Nicholas he replied that he didn't care is they enjoyed it and their parents were happy that they had something to do as the winter dragged on.

At the end of the first day she had spent much of the time trying to determine just which toy would be appropriate for her niece.

Then Lady Veronica spotted a small doll in the corner that had not been finished and it struck her that the poor thing had been abandoned. When she made inquiries they relayed to her that the doll was to be a present for a little girl in the Northern Province last year but that war and famine had taken its toll and the girl died before it could be finished. The boy who had started it just didn't have the heart to continue on so she was put over in the unfinished pile with some others. Once in a while a new recruit would work on one from that pile in order to develop his skills but they were never finished and in the end they wound up in the fire.

Lady Veronica was appalled at that as she could see the love and intensity that had been put into its creation so she selected that doll to be the one she would finish in the name of the young girls memory. As fate sometimes plays cruel jokes on humans the young girls name was Ann.

Since it was to be her first attempt Nicholas suggested she try out developing her skills on some other pieces first to get the hang of it. Once again as she set her mind to it she was able to bring out the best quality in unfinished work and restored several pieces. She knew that she had many months throughout the winter to work on the doll so she was in no hurry. She dedicated much of her time and effort in restoring old and abandoned toys to bring them to life. Most of those who observed her skills concluded that she had a lot of formal training as a perk to her position but in actuality she had only sparse exposure to wood arts and very little in the realm of colors. She had acquired most of her abilities by simply watching the skilled crafts-man of the countries where she visited.

On several occasions she had become so intense with her work that she skipped many meals and would work late into the night. Nicholas would find her hunched over a project and have to pull her away as the hour was very late and he had to close down the store.

It turned out to be a labor of love and she completely forgot time and the distribution of the gifts which always took place on Christmas week. She accompanied Nicholas and his friends in making the rounds. Once again many were surprised at the number of gifts that were avail-able for presentation. She had personally crafted twenty three and had started a small group who determined that unfinished work was not acceptable and helped her in completing and restoring an additional forty four pieces. Since some of the unfortunate families didn't have anyone to make toys for the young, Lady Veronica made sure that these young ones, even though some were not old enough to understand, were presented with a gift. Her outpouring of caring and love affected the entire township even more than that which Nicholas had started. It wasn't just a gift it was a special prize from the Lady of Royalty. Somehow it never affected her and she was always a lady with the special gift of humility.

"Oh, what a party!" she exclaimed as she observed the glee of the young and the sincere appreciation of the parents. "One couldn't ask for more unless of course it was with her own children. Nicholas leaned over and whis-pered "Perhaps you will have some of your own someday." She experienced a feeling that she had never encoun-tered before and it left her breathless. She had always known that someday she would have to get married and have her own but she never thought of it in that way. She knew she was expected to and she would in the proper time follow the established protocol but she never really looked forward to it as a joy of life.

"It's funny how things turn out." She said to herself. Somewhere in the middle of nowhere in the dead of winter with all poised at a standstill she had experienced a new sensation in life that would hold on to her for many years to come.

By the end of the evening she allowed that she had become infatuated with Nicholas. She thought of it as an abstract as he was not of royalty and she knew it was her responsibility to carry on the royal line. The thought of marring and settling down with a foreigner, a commoner none the less never entered her consciousness. At any rate she felt a stirring in her inner being and she determined to follow it wherever it was to wind up. *"Upon my return, I shall pursue the cause for which I was born."* Somewhere in her heart of hearts she knew that the time was coming.

The next morning Veronica arose to a beautiful sun filled day. The snow had fallen over the night and lay deep upon the marshes and the sides of the hills barely displayed their presents below the white fluff. It seemed that the winter decided that it was time and would wait no more. She wasn't dismayed by it as she knew it would come sooner or later and she would just deal with it. As the lady in waiting pushed back the heavy curtains that blocked the light while she slept a smile came to her face. "So this is the time we've all been waiting for?" She spoke aloud but not to anyone in particular. "This is the official first day of winter that has been spoken of. Look at all of its beauty, its breath taking." The Ladies in waiting just giggled and laid out her clothing for the day. As she looked at the arrangement of her wardrobe she decided that instead of the blue that she had selected the night before that she instead would elect to wear the red attire today. "*Somehow*," she told herself, "*it seems more appropriate.*" She never gave thought that Nicholas had mentioned that his favorite color was red. It just seemed appropriate for the day. After a leisurely breakfast she headed for Nicholas office intent on seeing if he was up and about. She had no doubt in her mind that he would be there as from the people she had encountered all of them spoke very highly of him and had address one of his most endearing attributes as promptness.

As Veronica approached the building she saw what seemed to be a very confusing sight. Smoke bellowed out of the top of the building and flames lapped through the broken windows. The volunteer fire fighters were attempting for all they were worth to contain the carnage as it swept close to the adjoining building. Without given thought as to her own attire or safety she plunged into the midst of the activity and started helping with the bucket brigade. She issued orders to her people to pull as many things as they could away from the infernal to rob it of its fuel and save whatever could be salvaged.

Once she had established control over her sector she determined that it was time to look to the injured. Veronica ordered her soldiers to continue to work under the command of the man in charge and took her ladies in waiting to the area where the wounded were being attended to. Several had burn injuries and a few were faint from the smoke that they had inhaled. She continued to work in that area for several hours until she was informed that the fire had been contained and much of the product in the adjoining stores had been salvaged thanks to her quick thinking and ability to organize a sector to thwart the advance of the fire. Finally after taking a toll of her people and determining that all of those affected by the fight were in stable condition she determined to sit and take a deep breath.

"What do you suppose caused this?" She inquired of one of the merchants. To her surprise his response was; "That infernal toy building in the back is where the fire started." The tone of his voice caused her to look at the man in a new light. Up to this point she had assumed that Nicholas was well liked by everyone in town. With some of the merchants gathering and murmuring amongst themselves she obtained a new perspective on just where the truth lay. They weren't large in number but never the less a significant number of people to set her mind to wondering if an under toe of discontent was brewing.

As she contemplated the issue she saw Nicholas arrive. He had been in the rear of the store when the fire broke out and it was nearly consumed by it. Since he never locked the doors of the toy store allowing anyone access as they willed, he was able to escape out the back. One thing that puzzled him though was that a large quantity of discarded wood had been piled up next to the door and he initially had a hard time clearing the path in order to escape. He said that he did not remember the pile being there when they finally closed up the night before. At first he thought that someone had come in early with the intent of helping to clear the area so the festivities could continue the next morning. After giving it some thought he said that perhaps someone had intentionally strewed the pile to block the exit of anyone caught in the store. Another thing that was odd was the fact that kerosene oil had been spilled over much of the place. This led him to believe that the fire was intentionally set. Lady Veronica resolved to keep her peace at this point but made a mental note as to who had been in the small crowd that the merchant had been speaking too. The one thing that Nicholas was happy about was that the celebration had been conducted yesterday and most of the gifts were already given out. "That was a God send." He commented. "Normally the celebration would not have been until tonight but with the weather forecast we decided to have it last night."

The remainder of the day was spent in attempting to recover as much of the materials that survived and sorting out that which was a total loss. Although much of the interior of the building had been scorched the frame of the building seemed to be intact. Over the next two days his attention was on as much recovery as possible. As luck would have it much of the front of the store where the books were kept was spared although there were a few sections that revealed that flammable liquid had been dispersed in one given area. At first the merchants were concerned about their records but when Nicholas informed them that a complete second copy was stored in a separate place in a building he had leased over two blocks away it relieved many of their concerns.

While speaking of the carnage and the untimeliness of it Lady Veronica sat quietly and listened. She made a mental note of those who seemed to be at odds with Nicholas, those who were simply confused and those who were ardent supporters. Although most of the supporters were merchants whose stores were not close to the fire she noticed that a couple of the disheartened ones were also away from the immediate area. They spent the better part of a week cleaning up the mess and one evening while she was dining with Nicholas she made it a point to reveal to him the events as she had seen them unfold. He was quite shocked at the names of some of those who had joined in the conversation. He had felt that both Ruddy, the cabinet maker and Thomas the window maker had always supported him. It didn't surprise him however that the instigator of the conversation was his neighbor on the main strip. He knew that Mr. Jablanksie, his neighbor had been in some financial trouble for the past couple of years and had resolved to speak to him about his negligence in not paying his back payments for services rendered. Mr. Jablanksie had taken that location a couple of years back in spite of Nicholas advise not to as the Hall Tree business was not really thriving and it could lead to financial difficulties. Now he was sure glad that he did keep a separate set of books as that was the very area where the fire was the most intense and reaped the most destruction. He kept this to himself though as it wouldn't be proper to discuss a client's finances even with the Lady Veronica. It wouldn't be until much later when he would be able to put it all together and then without reservation use it to defeat Mr. Jablanksie in a bid for the possession of mayor during the election cycle. For the time being he was content to make note of the facts as they presented themselves and formulate a solid case to present if this event ever became an issue.

Each day as the winter more firmly pursued its grip on the land and made the town totally isolated. Outside of the area the world became a haze but within the framework of the community life went on its merry way. By the end of the third week after the fire most of the damage had been recovered, except of course for the toy building. Since passage was blocked and no traffic was able to move except for within the town most of the merchants turned to their stores of wood and started making new products for the next spring. This was a time, although completely isolated from the rest of the world, to concentrate on the new ideas that they had been working on to further differentiate themselves from the world outside. Many had ideas stored in their hope chests and decided which ones they would attempt for the start of the new season come spring.

Lady Veronica woke up to a dreary day with dark clouds hanging low and the mist settled itself several inches above the ground. Up to this point total isolation had turned from enthusiasm to drudgery of the short cold days and the even colder lengthy nights. Sometimes the snow lay so deep that they were confined o their lodging for days at a time. Fortunately for Lady Veronica a door way had been cut from the sleeping quarters to the restaurant and they, knowing what was to come, had laid in an adequate supplies.

As she contemplated her lot she looked in vain to see if any relief was in the making. After a bit she observed what she thought were shadows in the mist. One at first then slowly as the fog lifted she could see several more. A twinge of excitement fluttered through her as she determined something definitely was out there. The presence of the barbaric Vikings of last year had faded into oblivion and she could feel the excitement growing as she called for her accompaniment and pointed out the activity. "Perhaps" she thought the long lost world was returning. She hurried to Nicholas store to see if anyone else had seen the objects although they were now gone. She joyfully opened his door to exclaim that she had seen activity on the hill side. She was initially was met with the blank stare of indifference as she perceived it to be. On a second look she could see that Nicholas was concentrating on the books before him and was not aware of anything going on outside his vision.

Once he realized who it was his continence changed as he featured a large smile. "Oh, I'm sorry" she said I didn't mean to disturb you."

"You're never a disturbance." he replied. "Just what is it you saw?" She explained how she had seen the shadows in the mist and was elated that perhaps the pass had been cleared. "Not likely.'" He replied, "Not this time of the year. But it's certainly worth looking into." They formed a small party of scouts to search the area and when they returned they brought the news that a Caribou and deer herd had passed close by and had continued their journey. This was good news as it meant the hunters could obtain some fresh meat. Nicholas as the mayor was officially in charge of getting the party ready. His duties were light though as the hunters were all experienced and knew what they needed to do.

Nicholas said that he wished that he could accompany them but as they were professionals and well equipped in stature and stamina he'd only be a hindrance to them. Besides his duties here required his presences so he allowed that fleeting thought to pass. A large gathering saw the hunting party off and wished them Gods speed as they disappeared into the fog. He, with a slight smile stated that he'd initially thought of going along but alas it was not to be as his physical make up could prove to be lacking and cause more harm than good. The Lady Veronica replied that she was sure that he would do well in the forest if need be as he had proven time and again that he has the ability to adapt. That evening while at supper she mentioned the idea again about obtaining the castle. He couldn't remember if anyone had laid claim to the territory but promised to look into the matter.

Three days later the hunters returned with five sleds of fresh meat. It would be enough for the entire town for some time. The snows, it seemed had spent its fury and perhaps the passes would be opened in short order. The merchants of course were happy as after all their work they now had an opportunity to get their wears to market.

As the time came Lady Veronica was conflicted over the two scenarios. One, she would love to stay here as the town had initially received her, first as royalty then later as a friend. However she knew that she had a responsibility to return so sadly she packed her belongings and prepared to leave with the first contingent. Some of the town folks told her that there would be at least four excursions during the summer and she didn't have to leave on the very first one. As tempting as it was she recognized that the longer she stayed the least likely it would be that she would leave at all. One of her escorts suggested that sometimes these trips took years and they really won't be expecting her back until she arrived. While the thought of it sounded intriguing she suspected that the longer she waited the harder it would be to let go.

Chapter 5

All things equal she was aware of her responsibilities so she packed and prepared to leave with the first departure. During her last days she was informed by Nicholas that he had researched the annuals as far back as he could and could not find any claim or lien on the property. Since there existed no national government as she had described in her home land the area was governed by the local regions and a regency was established by the leader proclaiming the title to the land. He said that he would send an enquiry to all of the surrounding towns to see if anyone had laid clamed to it. If no one would claim it as part of his regency then he would lay claim to it and they could work on establishing the renovations she was seeking. If a dispute were to arise over he claim he towns in question would work out an amiable agreement.

Since the old castle had been long ago vacated he doubted that anyone would have any interest in it so giving no complications he was sure he could lay claim to it and formalize an agreement when she could take possession. Although she knew that it would take some time she was already planning on her return trip to the area. She was aware that although her personal preference would be to report to the king and return on the very next ship available that things didn't always work out as she wished. So she resolved to complete her mission and make a report to the king.

As the caravan arrived at the castle for their final stop over as the last leg of their journey they found it occupied by a large contingent of Northerner's who insisted that they had received word that a foreigner was going to take their land and were prepared to defend their right to maintain it. When this information was relayed to Lady Veronica she immediately sent an emissary to those concerned professing that she had no intention to take away any lands that historically belonged to someone else. She arranged for a meeting with the Chief leader of the clan and expressed her desire to renovate the castle and establish trade to the benefit of all. Veronica was very specific in relaying her intent to recognize any and all legitimate claims and was looking forward to forming an alliance that would be beneficial to all.

At first her words fell on deaf ears as the chiefs of the clans proclaimed that they only did business with warriors of renown and definitely not with a female. While they were discussing the matter one of the chiefs who arrived late started screaming and carried no at the top of his lungs. When things finally calmed down he stated that she was the one who had bested his clan during the first encounter last fall and had caused him to lose no less than seventeen of his most fierce warriors and four of his best wolves. He had sworn at the time he would chase her to the ends of the earth if necessary to exact retribution. The warriors he wasn't very upset about they could be replaced. The wolfs on the other hand had been his since they were cubs and could never be replaced. While telling his story he started drawing his sword only to be met by three others who stood in front of her. The head chief flatly stated that she was under a flag of truce under his protection and his word would not be broken. Besides he reasoned if she has bested you in an assault it is commendable and will classify her as an honorable warrior of renown. That being the case he would hear what she had to say.

Lady Veronica laid out her plan for renovations of the castle and stated that now that she knew of the rightful owners she would use their shields to set up a place of honor for each deserving tribe. She received word that the ship that she originally transported on had left some ten days earlier and wouldn't be returning for a least another month. It worked out well in her mind as she would be able to delay her departure from this place and perhaps work a truce. When asked what was in it for them she very coyly stated that they would be able to get the things they need without losing their independence, establish a permanent base for their families and grow in wealth and stature while adding to their clan. This enticed several of the chiefs as their numbers had been dwindling for some time now and this would offer a way to replenish their clans.

She spent the next six days obtaining information that she'd need to insure her plans were consistent with the ideals of the tribes before departing to Points-Ville. She was able to negotiate plans that may prove fruitful. At one point during her stay she had the feeling that even though she was under the protection of the clans while here once she left the protected area she would be subject to attack by the one decenter. Using this as a premise she offered a challenge to the disgruntled chief. The high council stated that as long as she was under their protection he could not harm her but by issuing a challenge she had terminated that protective hand.

Since Lady Veronica had spent a lot of time in the archives during the past several days and replied that she was aware of the protocol and wished to invoke the seventh clause of the creed to allow her to select a protectorate. There was quite a bit of commotion about that as no one outside the clans had ever evoked their creed let alone a woman. Many stated that as an outsider she had no right to selectively use the creed. Others, while they had no objection to an outsider using the rule didn't know if it would apply to a woman. She was quick to point out that since she had already been accepted as a warrior of renown that logically it fell into place that she would be able to activate the warrior creed. Finally the discussion was over and it was agreed that she would be able to select her choice as a representative.

She acknowledged that she understood and was informed that she should select a fully qualified warrior because if her stand in were to loose he would lose his life and she in turn would forfeit hers also. She didn't hesitate for even a second. "I declare my stand in as the young warrior Klabith of the Keno tribe." This shocked everyone to the core. Klabith was the youngest son of the Keno leader and he had just been acknowledged as a full-fledged warrior. The leaders face went from a mile wide smile to a chalk white expression and a frown of concern.

"How can I be expected to kill my own child?" He blustered as he appealed to the council that this not be allowed. Once again a great commotion ensued and went on for hours. After a while and a lot of discussion it was determined that since they had granted her the right of exception they could also with the acquiescence of the plaintiff resolve the issue without spilling blood. That left the final decision squarely in his court. If his hatred was so intense he could kill his own son then she felt her life would be at an end without hope anyway. She had studied the creed carefully and was sure with one of his own line of succession that was to be terminated at his own hands that the leader would in turn place the sword upon himself. While his hate for her was strong she was counting on the bond of blood to be even tighter.

The young warrior was well aware of the situation and stepped forward with his sword drawn and pointed it to himself. I will settle this for my father he stated.

"STOP!" shouted the father "your sacrifice would be in vain as it would not count as you would not be killed in battle."

"Then slay me and avenge your honor" the young man replied. The father dropped his sword and swore before the entire assembly that he would drop his petition. The entire place broke out in cheers and the celebration went on deep into the night. Some were still singing when the dawn peeked over the mountain.

Lady Veronica made sure to seek out the aggrieved chief who had renounced his claim and offered that upon her return she would bring back the pride of the hunting dogs from the line of her king. This suited him well and he was satisfied that everything was turning out even better than he expected. He was honored that she had bothered to seek him out and this would appease the gods for the loss of his wolfs. She stayed another six days before returning to Points-Ville and was satisfied that she was able to instigate some of the preliminary negotiations, many of which were fruitful.

Upon her arrival in Points-Ville Lady Veronica wrote a lengthy letter to Nicholas explaining what she had found out and the agreements she was able to come by while with the tribes. She indicated that she hoped that all was well with him and perhaps they would meet again next year, or baring orders from the king by his decree of an assignment she was sure she could get back at least in two years.

Once again she sat before an empty page. Once again she was torn between what she knew to be true love for Nicholas and her obligations to her king. Finally she spelled out the words and knew somehow placing them on paper solidified her intent. Veronica didn't know how, but she knew it was going to happen.

As she spent her time waiting on the ship to return she put an emissive amount of it in getting to know more of the town people much like she did in Oy-Land. She seemed to have a natural appeal to all she met and in short order became a well-known name. Not just a name of royalty but one who could help in a crisis and trusted to keep her word whenever she saw fit to inject herself into a situation. As a gregarious individual she was always stepping her foot forward in offering help. When the people heard about the lengths that she had gone through during the fire at Oy-Land and that she had actually participated in the fight both at the castle and when the caravan had been attacked her fame spread rapidly. The fact that she was able to contact the barbarians was regarded as a small miracle in and of itself.

On one occasion she heard of a family with seven small children who had met with hard times and sent her escort to see what could be done to help. The father had been severely injured during the early spring while hunting. As the story was told he had run across a young family in the wilderness who were completely lost. They did not speak the language very well and he had a hard time deciphering exactly what the problem was. While he was offering his services the couple hit him over the back of the head, stole his money, such as it was and left him for dead in the wilds. While he was still drogue he was attacked by a huge black bear who nearly chewed his arm off. The wife went into early labor lost her new born and died that same day. Now there were seven orphans with a one armed father who was trying to survive. Lady Veronica didn't hesitate and went directly to the home. She had her ladies in waiting to assist in setting up the house and insured that there was enough food and clothing to provide a safe environment for the children. He was attempting to recover on his own as he had no money and could not pay doctor bills and such. Not even giving it a second thought she sent for the doctor. She gave him the equivalent of twenty pieces of gold in a certificate although she didn't have the actual gold left. Her note was accepted as everyone accepted her word as honorable.

Finally the ship arrived and she was met by an emissary form the king. He had been informed of all the good work that she was doing and although he didn't like nor trust the barbarians he placed his seal on the document of acceptance and had furnished sufficient amount of gold to pay all the debts and establish a reserve. It seemed that her efforts not only were hailed as her being a great and wonderful person but also it was extended to the king. He of course delved in the acknowledgement of his graciousness and expressed his pride that one of his own had accomplished so much in so little time. Lady Veronica took this as a compliment and stated that she felt good to have served the king and display his great honor. Little did she know the chastisement she would get in private upon arrival back in the kingdom.

Under his breath he resolved to take her to task for the use of the crown without explicit permission and verbatim guidance from his majesty. The king held a tight rein on all of his ambassadors and insisted on approving every line of every agreement. This had caused troubles in the past as everything had to be written, sent back to the homeland, personally approved by the king and then returned. In some instances some simple adjustment to an agreement would take several months. On one occasion in the southlands of the African continent a war raged for more than a year while they awaited the approval of a simple addition of a line of context that offered water rights to a local village. No one, of course would ever say anything that would cause the king distress so these sorts of things so they simply were just not reported. The fact that several thousand people were sacrificed to sooth his ego was never mentioned in his presence. For the time being though she was satisfied that she had done what is correct and was happy as she was led to believe that he was pleased.

The ship where she was scheduled to return on had met with a hard journey and had to undergo extensive repairs before it could set sail again. Lady Veronica however wasn't distressed over the delay as she was enjoying the landscape and had even returned to the castle on one occasion to oversee the renovations. A second caravan had arrived and she received the word that negotiations were preceding nicely. By the time she actually was able to leave the country it was well into the summer. Several communications had transpired as she was now writing entire letters in complete detail almost every day about the progress. As the summer wore on she at one point received as part of her message that perhaps she should stay and continue to oversee the project. This thrilled her of course but upon closer investigation of the content she could see the underwriting on the letter that indicated that the king was not actually giving her permission nor did he expect that she would actually take that route. That was her first inclination that something was not right and that it would be in her best interest to return post haste.

Finally the day came. The morning sun shown off the water and the wind was so calm it was almost as if there was no wind at all. This did not deter the captain though as he had been sailing for many years and was both familiar with the currents and the prevailing winds once they had rounded the point and were on the open sea. Lady Veronica wondered at it all as she would have guessed that something in the way of a wind, any wind at all had to show itself before the ship would leave the harbor. None the less the ship lifted its anchor on time and started what seemed to be adrift. Actually the tide was going out so it pulled the structure out to sea. As planned once they cleared the point and were in the open the wind picked up and they were able to set sail. She met the old sailor that she had helped on her madden voyage and he relayed how he had run into a stroke of good fortune since he'd last met her. He had been able to obtain a new ship, new to him anyway through a benevolent unnamed donor and it was in the process of being upgraded and refitted right now. He mentioned that she had been the one to relight his desires to make his dreams come true and within a few months he'd be his own captain. She secretly smiled at the thought of having helped him.

Later that day they were met by a whaling boat. It had been out for some time and wanted to exchange some oil for food that might be on the ship. The captain being an old salt expected this to happen and had extra cargo on hand. The food and sail materials were not very expensive when managed up against the oil that they carried as the oil was always in demand and food on the other hand would spoil before they reached their destination. The old sailor told the Lady Veronica that in his refitting of his vessel he had reconstructed it to have a double hull to prevent taking on water when the outer planks were broken during storms and such. She said she had never thought to do something like that but now that he mentioned it, it made sense. "Actually" he acknowledged to her that it was not his original idea but when he had been speaking to a very young Norseman; he had related the idea as he, even at his young age, had seen several vessels lost due to the sides of the ships being punctured during the fierce north ice storms. Twice he had been on one of those ships and almost lost his life. The death toll for that area was great and old sailors didn't seem to stay long. The older they got the more likely they were to steer south. Sometimes the storms took the ships to the bottom of the sea but at least the water was warmer and the possibilities of surviving were much greater.

The Lady made a mental note to perhaps address this issue with the king if ever she had the opportunity. They continued without incident for the next several days. The mornings were bright, the wind was brisk and the temperature was pleasant. One morning she was watching the dolphins swim close to the ship dodging in and out of the wake. She had just grabbed a hold of a rope that hung to secure the sails when the entire ship was jarred. The entire rear end where the ruder had been was ripped off as if it had been hit by an ax. Planks and large chunks of beams were flying everywhere. In short order the captain ordered all passengers to the dinghies and the sailors assigned insured that as many as could be accounted for were boarded. Lady Veronica was separated from her normal accompaniment and placed in a small boat with only two other passengers and two sailors. As she looked around she could see a shore line not too far off in the distance and could tell immediately that they were headed in that direction. They reached the shore line in less than an hour and she peered out to sea to see if she could glean any information as to what might have happened.

One of the young sailor stated that they had been attacked by Moby Dick a sea monster that was known to shred ships. He had never believed it before but he had gotten a glimpse of the creature and was sure it was at least as big as the ship they were on and perhaps even bigger. He told her not to worry though as it would never come this close to the land and they were prepared for this in the event things went array. As they unloaded the contents of the survival boat they noticed activity in the brushes and along the tree line. "Oh, Oh" one young sailor let out a sigh of exasperation. I think we've been spotted. "Isn't that good?" The Lady replied. "Perhaps you're Ladyship but perhaps not. They are not always friendly. Just stay behind us and we'll protect you." She thought for a moment then said "No we will form a defensive circle and each of us will assist the other. I just wish I had my sword." We have an extra one in the boat" he replied and she sorted through the reserves to obtain it. In short order each of the five were armed and readied themselves for whatever may come their way. The sailor in charge seemed to be very young and unsure of himself so she, without reservations took charge.

First let's gather as much as we can and get to the safety of the trees. If we can find a place where we can defend from a limited number of sides we'll be better off.

Chapter 6

They gathered as much as they could carry in hopes of obtaining enough food and weapons to sustain them for a short while in the event they were attacked. Once they reached the tree line they determined that they could perhaps find some sort of natural shelter. As luck would have it they encountered a large area where fallen trees were piled up higher than the head and was only open on one side. At first they viewed it as a God send but quickly realized that it had two very distinct draw backs. One there was no back door to escape out of if it became necessary, and two they couldn't see what was on the other side so they didn't know if a potential enemy would be able to clime atop; the fallen timber and gain the upper hand by shooting down on the defenders. Quickly they determined that it would be a death trap and left that area.

When they looked back to the sea they spotted another small boat pulling up next to theirs and at first thought it must be others from the ship. It didn't take long to determine that the other boat was not of their accompaniment and their intent was to take what had been left behind. Lady Veronica yelled at the top of her lungs and led a charge back to their boat. The others were so astounded by the commotion that they quickly abandoned their quest and determined that it would be in their best interest to vacate the premises. Those from the other boat quickly recessed into the trees and didn't seem to be coordinated enough to launch a counterattack. Once the five arrived at their boat and secured it Lady Veronica called out to them. We do not want your provisions. You may return and depart in peace if you are of a mind to be civil. Slowly the small group raised their heads out of the area where they were hidden and hesitantly returned to the shore. As it turned out it was four young people, two males and two females none of whom seemed to be past their adolescences yet.

When Lady Veronica saw who it was, she changed her tone as her protective instincts kicked in. With a much calmer voice she asked who they were and just what were they doing here in the middle of nowhere? The tallest boy looked at her and in a shaky voice replied that they had been on a ship that had suffered a similar fate as theirs and was forging for survival. The two girls, one of them very young, couldn't have been more than eight, just stood there with their heads down whimpering "Please don't kill us." "Not to worry" The Lady replied. You are now under the protective custody of the King of England. We'll see to it that you are returned to your proper place." "We don't have a place anymore" the older girl said in a whimper so low that it was almost inaudible. Lady Veronica considered that for a few seconds then replied "Well you do now. You'll all be guest of the kings' castle when we arrive home." The smaller boy simply shook his head no and replied "The king of England is our enemy." "Perhaps" the Lady replied, but until you have a chance to return to your home land you can consider this a truce between you and the crown." Nothing more was said on the matter.

Now let's get things organized and see just what is next. They had completely forgotten those peeking through the tree line as they first arrived. Lady Veronica asked if the kids knew anything about them and the older boy replied that they had been captured by them for a couple of days before they made their escape. Whoever they were they didn't speak English and he thought they were from the north tribes. She decided to test her skills in the new language she had learned while a guest in the Viking camp. She started with a greeting addressing herself as a member of the clan of Keno tribe from across the sea. She wasn't making up a story as she had been officially made a member of the tribe while she had stayed at the castle. The Keno chief actually gave indications that he had grown a liking to her and dubbed her the first female warrior of honor that had ever been named.

After a short while a big burley man who stood at least six foot four and stood head and shoulders over her stepped out into the open. "Who dares to mention the keno tribe?" He inquired. "I, the wolf slayer" was her reply. That had been given her as an official name out of respect for his pet wolf. The man seemed to be confused at first then demanded the proof. "Gladly" she replied as she pulled the paw of the wolf that was hanging beneath her tunic. "The wolf was an honorable friend and now serves as my protectorate." The warrior stood for a short period looking perplexed. "I have heard of the story, but I figured you to be at least ten feet tall from the story." She had to laugh at that. Perhaps the story had grown as the character did. It seemed to be the way of it among all people. The longer the story is repeated the larger the victor becomes.

Finally he nodded and extended his spear towards her. No harm shall come to the Lady of the wolf slayer or her party. All of this was spoken in their native Tung and his tone left no doubt that she and her party was under the protection of this chief. She could tell by his stature and his adornment that he was a chief and perhaps a top chief in the clan. She explained how they had been passing peacefully through the straits when they were attacked by the biggest whale she had ever seen. "Moby Dick" he replied. She noticed that he was missing part of his left hand but didn't mention it. He lifted it in pride and retold the story of how Moby Dick had attacked his small vessel and how he single handedly had chopped off part of its nose although it cost him several fingers. "Better a few fingers he recanted then my whole being. They escorted the landing party to the village some few miles from the shore. "We will scan the beaches tomorrow to see if anyone else survived. But I doubt it." It seems this particular whale had distaste for the vessels that transported through this area. The roomer was that a British captain had once sailed this area looking for the big monster so he could mount him in his front yard.

Later that evening after the supper meal the warriors were sitting around the fire and each in turn would tell a tale of how they had bested their enemy in battle and had won the red ribbon they had tied to their hair. It seemed everyone was enjoying themselves until it came around to Lady Veronica. She gracefully passed to the next saying that her deeds were nothing compared to the great warriors of honor that sat about the fire. One young warrior called out that she had to do so in the name of their favorite god and in the name of the chief who had bestowed upon her the honor of an honorable warrior and presented her with her name and the gift of the wolfs foot. Lady Veronica tried to make it short and bestowed great accolades on the chief and his faithful wolf. She tried to make it known that it wasn't her great strength but her ability to use what she had in the strength of her comrades. Although, she said that she had been the one recognized for her cunningness it was actually a collective effort on the part of all who were with her. This didn't set well with the warriors and they were making their displeasure known to the chief.

The head clansman was placed on a spot and had to rectify the situation readily or the disgruntled of the clan would make an issue of it. He came up with an idea and inquired why she did not wear the red ribbon if it had been presented to her at all. The answer would only lie in her revealing the secret word which was only known by those who had been bestowed that honor. She took her time and slowly circled the group. As she passed by the two sailors and one other of her group she whispered to be ready for a fight. She pointed out the two biggest men standing in front of the pole and instructed her people to be ready to strike when she called out "TO ARMS." They were perplexed and attempted to ask why this was to be but she just replied you have to trust me and if you fail to get those two right away we will all loose our lives.

As she completed the half circle and approached the chief she responded; "I will reveal the word to you but not in public as there are those here that should not hear it. We'll retreat to the logs over there and I will whisper it to you." "You are a very wise person" he replied. "There are those here that should not know it. So she led the way to the wood pile. When she arrived she pulled him close and inquired "Why do you wear the red ribbon on the left shoulder rather than the right?" Before he could even attempt to answer she thrust her sword into his midsection.

"TO ARMS" she cried. As she did she thrust a shiv into the nearest enemy and with a half swing thrust her sword deep into the shoulder of the next one. The three that she had assigned to dispatch the two warriors had managed to work their way around to the back side of each and when the call came launched their surprise attack killing both immediately. Most of the remainder of the warriors were very drunk and had a hard time getting started. The battle such as it was lasted but a short time and all who were about the circle had been killed. She commanded that the torches be set on all of the camp and all resistance was to be met with immediate death to the oppressors. Once the battle was finished and the camp completely destroyed Lady Veronica gave the orders to return to the beach and set up a defensive position in case any of those who had escaped would attempt to launch a counterattack.

They had taken all they could carry in the way of food and weapons and established a defensive position where they had their backs to the sea and they were on a narrow strip where access would be limited to at the very best on two sides. As they settled down for the night the one sailor who had been in charge initially asked her what that was all about. They seemed so friendly and we were sure we were secure at least for the night.

Lady Veronica replied that they had all worn their red

ribbon over their left shoulder. At first she thought that it might be because they were across the sea from the others but as she thought on it she became suspicious and delved deeper into her memory. She remembered the code of the clan and the meaning of the red band across the right shoulder. The more she thought on it the more convinced that something was wrong. The straw that broke the camel's back was when the chief stated that she needed to reveal to them the word of the creed. In her short time with her teacher he had cautioned that no true warrior of the clan would ever ask for the word of the law in front of any one. At that point she knew that what had been gnawing at the back of her mind was the fact that these were imposters. She also knew if she were to give the answer to him her entire group would immediately be destroyed. She was left with only one option and that was to strike first.

As the sun rose over the tree line the guards awakened her with the news that one more dinghy had been spotted and they were sending a party of three to gather them so they could make a larger force. Throughout the day they scoured the shore line and found four more small boats that had managed to make it to shore. Now with a small fleet of seven boats and some thirty four personnel they were able to establish a plan to precede down the coast line and towards a small village that one of the sailors new about. They spent one extra day searching in the northerly direction to see if anyone else had made it but were unable to locate any further survivors. They lashed the dinghies together and stuck close to the shore line. They had enough equipment to conduct proper fishing excursions and were close enough to the shore line that they could forge for berries and hunt small animals. This went on for three days and she was able to meet up with the sailor who had originally taken her fancy and he of course took command. Lady Veronica didn't take offense to that as she was relieved that she no longer was responsible for the survivors and could concentrate on helping the sick and wounded.

On the evening of the third day while they were sitting around after the meal hour she asked what would provoke the whale who had attacked the ship and how many lives were lost. The sailor stated that the captain knew the risk but had opted to take that route as the report was that a large gale had been spotted and he didn't want to be caught on the open sea when it arrived. He had cautioned the captain about these waters but he wouldn't hear of it. What he didn't take into account was that they had traded for the whale oil and this particular whale had no love for those who killed his fellow clansmen so to speak. If they had not had the oil onboard they might have passed safely through the straits and bypassed the storm at the same time. As it turned out he paid the price for his foolishness, one that the sailor would never make again.

For the next week they progressed southward keeping close to the shore and hunting whenever they had a chance. One day he came up to her and said that they would be in the village within the week and that he had sent two men on ahead to prepare the town for their arrival. They were a friendly lot but didn't like surprises and would certainly initiate a fight if this group just descended upon them. For the next three days they continued down the same direction and on the fourth they were met by a contingent of twenty armed men who were quite capable of launching an all-out battle. As they came closer the sailor yelled out

"høy en" the Norwegian name that translates to Tall One in English. He was easy to pick out as he was the tallest one in the group and the most fearsome looking.

"Broren sjømann (brother sea monster)" he responded with a great smile. The reunion was joyous and boisterous while each tried to outdo the other in their boasting. Lady Veronica just sat quietly by and watched as the groups merged with the survivors and each in turn were taken into their custody as a favorite.

As was the custom each of the towns' folks would sponsor one or two of the survivors and all were welcomed as a family of the supporter. It never dawned on her why she had not been selected until the sea monster as he was referred to raised her arm and declared her as his own sister.

As it turned out he had boasted of her and at first glance everyone knew without a doubt that she was the one that he had bragged on. When he took her into his home he introduced her to his wife and seven children and announced that this is the lady that he had told everyone about and that she had a special place in his home as his sister.

They rested for three days and nights as the celebration went on. Lady Veronica was treated as royalty not in the sense of her actual title but as one especially attended to and received the adoration of the entire community.

As the activities died down on the third night Lady Veronica approached her host. "While it's been a great time here I must now ask your leave as we are still in need of reporting back to the king and determining what next I must do before I can return to my new home. She quite astounded herself by identifying the place where she had left so short ago as her new home. The sea monster agreed and told her he would make arrangements for the group to continue their mission. He had horses available and determined that it would be the fasted and most direct route.

"It's not without danger" he concluded, "but then nothing is." So for the next five days they traveled from village to village to insure they were not accosted by the lawless. They were always received with great fanfare as massagers were sent ahead to inform the locals of their pending arrivals. As they entered one township they noted that most of the town people seemed to be nervous and shied away from them.

Her ambassador, being knowledgeable of the customs immediately reported that something was array. Lady Veronica as the leader of the group decided to go on through the town and make it know that they were going to camp a few miles closer to the next township. They made a special effort to appear to establish a camp for the night. In truth she had been down this road before and knew exactly what to expect. She had a small contingent set up fires and a makeshift camp while the main body of marines were split in a V formation and lay quietly awaiting the expected assault. The marine commander was a captain who had weathered many battles and knew exactly what was expected. The trap was set and everyone hunkered down.

Sure enough just as the moon came over the horizon the bandits launched their surprise attack. There was a surprise alright but it was not on the part of the traveling party. It seemed that the battle no sooner got off the ground then the trap was sprung and short order was made of the impending onslaught.

The loss of life on the part of the attackers was counted as 32 dead 17 severely wounded and several with minor wounds had been taken into custody. As for the defending force not even one reported a scratch.

The next morning Lady Veronica returned to the town and presented them with the bootie that they had collected off the bandits. This time they were greeted with cheers and a promise to provide information whenever the bandits were around again.

The rest of the journey was quiet and they made good progress towards their destination. Three days later they were met by a detachment of the kings' guard and escorted back to the palace.

Chapter 7

"Mrs. Nicholas Claus, that rings happiness in my ears as I contemplate as our time comes near".

Veronica had mailed and received a chest full of memories over the past year. Her devotion and determination to become Mrs. Claus had depended with each passing day. As she was reflecting on her latest ambassadorship assignment to Ireland and the culmination of this assignment her feelings of anticipation grew.

The king had a special interest in making a treaty with the Irish as there had been reports of pirate ships pillaging the east coast. Since she had studied the Irish language and especially the Gallic dialect she had naturally become the logical choice. Since the king had promised her time to return to her beloved upon completion of the assignment she was extremely happy that she would be able to report a successful mission.

"I'm sure the king will be pleased that his eastern border will be secure from the ruffians and piracy that have been raiding the cost land." Lady Veronica had not only managed an alliance with the proctor of their western lands to seek out and destroy the barbaric factions but

also to initiate the beginnings of a trade relationship that had gone array.

Things, it seems went from bad to worse in recent years had dropped from a tenuous acceptable coexistence to complete hostilities. Lady Veronica was able to convince the leaders that it was in their interest to form a bond and reopen trade allowing a mutual beneficial existence for all.

"*Yes*" she said to herself "*the king will be most pleased. And as for me …*" her thoughts were interrupted as she became aware that the crew had swung into battle mode. The anguish of mortal man became apparent as their wounds displayed that while negations had been successful not all was well on the eastern front.

Without hesitation she guided the wounded toward the make shift aid station and started tending to their wounds. The battle was short lived as her slower but larger ship was able to take advantage of their disguise. They sported the look of a merchant ship flying under the kings flag but was actually a military vessel fully loaded with troops and more than adequate fire power to repel even the best of the black flags with skull and cross bones.

As it happened this particular aggressor was not the cream of the croup and was subdued in short order. The kings ship thrust open the disguised trap doors and fired a broad side volley of fourteen cannons in to the side of the opposition. With its side laid wide open like the flesh on a side of beef she took on water rapidly. Her crew, even though they were seasoned warriors was taken completely by surprise and the command to abandon ship came in short order.

Most of them were killed in the fracas leaving only six

remaining and all were wounded. The lieutenant wanted to erect a gallows immediately and be done with it. The Captain of the guard although a young officer ordered that they have their wounds tended to and that they be placed in the brig.

When the impetuous lieutenant voice an objection the captain displayed restraint at his disappointment that his orders were questioned, gently pulled the junior officer off to the side and explained that as long as they lived the possibility of obtaining information pertaining to where they berthed and other information that could prove useful.

As it turned out two of the captives were very young. They were barely in their teens yet. Both were cabin boys and both served unwillingly their masters. Once this became apparent Lady Veronica recommended that the two be separated from the rest as they would be more likely to talk if they didn't feel intimidated by the older crew members.

As they were being led away one of the crew members yelled "If you talk to them I'll cut your throats. He added a few choice vulgar phrases and swore a curse upon them if they were to speak.

Both of the boys cowered as they were led away. The fear of the curse hung heavy on their minds and they were not in any physical or mental condition to talk.

There was a room adjoining Lady Veronica. The port holes were boarded shut and all items that could be conceivably used for escape or for a weapon were withdrawn from the room. The ship had been constructed originally with two doors with a small hall between to allow for couples to enjoin during a voyage but since there were no couples aboard the rooms had been renovated to accompany Lady Veronica. She offered the second room as a holding area as she had not really used it. Besides she reasoned she could look after the two lads and she was sure in her mind that given time she would be able to establish a certain amount of trust, relive the fears of the two and perhaps establish a display of kindness that would lead to some information.

In her formidable training years she developed the use of not only the Irish language but also several dialects. As it happened, these two spoke a version of Gallic that was generally unfamiliar with the formally trained translators of the realm. After all, as the thought patterns went, what would an officer of the crown gain by conversing with a common low life. Lady Veronica however became intrigued at an early age and had the good fortune to have a lady in waiting that severed as her mentor and enthralled her young mind with the tales of her home land.

She knew that it would take some time but since they were taking the long rout around the southern tip of the island it would be quite a while before they would dock. She made sure that the two had their wounds dressed and that they were as comfortable as possible given their circumstances. She always tried to keep the conversation light and as more information came out she would try to find ways to address them. As an example one day taller of the two youths mentioned the port of Biscuits on the eastern side of Ireland. She looked up that information on the maps available and found that it was close to the village of Hawthorn. She thought back on some of her lessons that she had enjoyed with her mentor and remembered that she had come from that region. With that in mind later that day she mentioned the name of the village and observed as the shorter one's eyes lighted up.

"I've always wanted to visit that area." She proclaimed as my Lady in Waiting Virginia had come from there. She could see the tears well up in the young ones eyes and decided that although she would not pursue it for the moment that she would look for an opening and address it again.

Later that evening as she passed by the room where they were being held she could hear crying from the room. She slowly opened the door to see the shorter one lying on the bed while the other one obviously older was attempting to calm the younger one down.

"What have we here?" Lady Veronica inquired.

"He's dyeing" the older boy replied. "He's bleeding and it won't stop.

"Let's take a look." Lady Veronica relied. "You tell the guard to bring a basin of water and some padding and we'll do what is needed to stop the bleeding." As she turned the young one over she discovered that he wasn't a he at all and compassion overcame her as she wrapped the girl in her arms and reassured her that she wasn't going to die.

After she was cleaned up and given a few facts of life Lady Veronica had her moved into her private quarters.

"I always knew there was something different about her." The older one stated.

"But I'd have never guested she wasn't a boy." I just thought since she was younger and weaker that she would just have to grow if she survived long enough. If they had known she was a female it would have been even harder. I'm sure after they rapped her and she was no longer of any use they would have just thrown her overboard."

Lady Veronica agreed and redoubled her intent to

protect the two. She had to smile at the thought that as tragic as it was the young girl Trish had gone through the experience with no preparation or advice from a woman as she had been totally unprepared for her change in life.

Late that night Lady Veronica was awaken to the quiet sobs of the girl. She picked the girl up and held her in her arms while she sang a lullaby of the Gallic marsh and the quiet clear nights. After a while the girl fell off to sleep and the Lady Veronica simply lay next to her and comforted her in her arms.

The next morning, while on deck enjoying the warm southern breeze the Lady Veronica once again mentioned the village of Hawthorn. She explained how she was familiar with the area. Trish at first recoiled as the sounds of the threat of the other captive returned to her mind.

"I can't speak about this or he will cut out my tong." The fear was very intense and her eyes widened as she contemplated her folly.

"Not to worry." Lady Veronica stated as she comforted her, "You will no longer be bothered by the likes of them. They can no longer harm you." The girl sobbed and replied "But you don't understand. They hold my entire family hostage and will enslave all of those they do not kill if I don't return with them." Her emotions were such that it was hard to understand her over the sobbing.

"You don't have to fear him. He will never return to tell the others." Trish simply slumped to the deck and cried. "You don't understand, you just don't understand. They live by a code and if he doesn't return the others will slay the very young, the crippled and the old and take the remainder as slaves.

Lady Veronica was appalled at the barbarism of it

and decided to ask the ship's captain if anything could be done. His initial reply was that even though it was a crime there wasn't anything he could do.

By that time they had rounded the southern tip of the English coast and were just a few days from port. She knew there was nothing she could do in the immediate future but it laid heavy on her mind and she resolved to talk to Virginia, her Lady in waiting and her esteemed mentor to see if she could glean any information that might be helpful. Since she had two days to think over the matter she started developing a plan for rescue.

Upon arrival from the Port of Biscuit they were greeted with a grandiose celebration and she reported her successes to the king. He was especially pleased that a bargain had been struck to thwart the pirates on his eastern coast and that she had been able to establish the ground work for a trade agreement. Since she had time to weave the thoughts of striking at the pirates on their home turf into the report she presented a creditable attack plan on the Port of Biscuits to bring the pirates low. He noticed her enthusiasm for the project and asked her to explain. As she unraveled the tale she tried to present it as a plan to assist the Irish Vector and destroy the infestation that bothered both Ireland and the British Empire.

The king quizzed her further and determined that there was more at stake then what was on the surface so he pondered on it.

"Given your great interest for this, I expect you'll want to be a part of it." She knew that he saw right through her play and decided to relay the entire story and of her desire to aid Trish and her family. The boy Paul had sworn allegiance to the crown in order to enter the service of the king. After all he reasoned he had never really know anything but misery from the country of his birth as he had served as a slave cabin boy as far back as he could remember.

The four adults had been tried and properly hanged and his only references to the past now were the kindness of Lady Veronica. Since he had sworn allegiance to the crown she had taken him as a confident and a researcher. He was assigned the task of learning to read and write. He proved to be a quick learner and was well versed in reading maps. As the chief slave cabin boy he had served the captain of the last two ships and had access to the captains' maps. They always intrigued him and his memory was sharp so he proved helpful to his captains.

He served them as best he could but always had it in mind to beak free one day and return to his home port, perhaps as a captain himself.

For now of course things were different and with the help of Lady Veronica as his superior he made the best of his situation and concentrated on learning all he could. His original intent never wavered though and he made no bones about it when he discussed it with the Lady. He vowed that his allegiance would always be and he'd never go back on his word.

After giving this some thought the king called Lady Veronica back to council.

"I see your desire to help these young people and although I'd like to help there is nothing I can do at the present. With the harsh winter setting in the thought of sending a fleet to the eastern side of Ireland is out of the question. With the harsh storms coming from the north to send a fleet out now would be a fool's errand. Besides by the time we would be able to get there he deed of total destructions would already be done."

Lady Veronica asked permission to speak and when granted proposed that the bad weather would also delay any executions as the barbarians would simply conclude that when the ship didn't return it was most probably moored somewhere awaiting the calmer spring. He king thought on that for a bit then replied "Be that as it may, I thought you'd want to return to your north land across the channel to your betrothed."

She smiled that special winning smile that would melt the heart of any man and simply stated that while that was her ultimate goal, life presents us with challenges that we had not prepared to meet yet life simply goes on. She would send the word to Nicholas that she had been delayed again and was certain that he would understand.

The king, realizing that further objections were useless decided to grant her permission to form a fleet and upon the advice of the military commanders they should sail on the first date in the spring that they determined would meet her demands with the best chance of success.

As Lady Veronica was popular with the naval officers she proceeded to inquire as to who would volunteer so as to avoid conscription. She found it easy to obtain the ships necessary as one of the chief military advisors was especially fond of her as she had intervened on several occasions on his behalf on his way up the ladder and greased the skids that enabled him to advance so rapidly. By the time she was finished she had a dozen ships lined up making repairs and ready to sail.

One day the king called her in and stated that if she

kept this up she would have his entire fleet going to Ireland in the spring.

"The Irish will probably think I've launched an invasion force." He said with a slight smile. His light heartedness allowed her to know that she wasn't in any real trouble.

"I've dispatched a courier to the reagent in charge of that province and explained our plans to assist him in routing out the infestation of that area. I'm sure he'll agree and we won't have any problems. What I've called you in for is I have a naval officer by the name of Horatio who is familiar with Ireland and its ports along the cost. More importantly he is an ardent meteorologist and a student of the north storms that occur during the winters. He claims that you don't have to wait the winter out.

Of course he only has six ships at his command and I'm not inclined to add any to it. So if you want to go now you'll have six ships on your quest. If you'd prefer to wait until spring and early summer you can have all twelve that you requested."

As she contemplated the wheels started to spin and a twinkle came into her eye.

"What do you have in mind?" The king asked. She promptly replied

"We should leave with the ships that are available and come spring you can, if it suits your purpose, dispatch the second half of the fleet. It will not only keep the pirates at bay but by the time the relief column arrives we should have enough information to launch even more strikes permanently destroying their ability to harass our eastern shores." The king smiled and replied "I like the way you think."

The next morning she reported to Admiral Hershel

with her small entourage that consisted of her chief lady in waiting Virginia, Paul as her interpreter, Trish who had acclimated well into becoming a young lady and a private escort of twenty four volunteer marines, all of whom were taking lessons in the Gallic language dialect. The Admiral introduced her to Vice Admiral Horatio and released her to his command. As the tide was on its way out, just as planned they set sail.

The day was brisk and the winds steady so they were able to make good time heading south. Once they reached the open sea and established a formation the Vice Admiral called a meeting of the staff. Included of course was Lady Veronica who was met with enthusiastic support as most of the officers had met her already and those who had not have a personal knowledge of her had heard the stories of her exciting past.

"We'll reach the southern tip by night fall" he began "and allow the southern currents to allow us to swing around the tip. We'll be well on our way by daybreak." He laid a map before them that displayed several course directions that they were expected to take and announced that he expected to arrive at the Port of Lisbon on the British cost by the end of the week.

Lisbon was a thriving port with a military garrison. He had sent word by land that he expected to arrive in five days and the commander of the garrison was to lie in supplies for them to enable them to continue their assignment.

"According to our weather forecasters we'll not run into any rough travel on this first leg of our travel, but on the other hand, it's that time of the year so keep alert. Storms can rise up without warning and if we are lax in our preparations we could lose a ship or two. I fully expect each ship's captains to remain vigilant and keep an eye out for each other.

With the exception of one, the rest of the ships were manned by seasoned officers and well weather worn crews. The last one, though it was his first command as captain was a seasoned first lieutenant and had the confidence of all the others. He had served under two of the other captains and had been recommended for the job when his captain had received severe injuries.

As four bells rang announcing the completion of the southern correction the sails were shifted to accommodate the new head winds. The original intent was to stick close to the shore line as possible to take advantage of the land mass that jutted out to the north and to remain in relatively calm waters.

Since Mother Nature takes no commands from a mere mortal man she pushed an early storm directly into their path. The currents and ferocious wind was pushing the fleet dangerously close to the rock formations so they headed for the open sea. The remainder of he day was a continuous struggle for control as they attempted to keep the six in some sort of a formation close enough to assist if need be yet not so close they'd ram each other when the two waves sent them hurling onwards towards each.

After sixteen hours of struggle they finally got the break they were looking for and just as the wild winds came without announcement they subsided. The crews were worn to a frazzle yet they dare not relax their guard as you never know when the old lady as they referred to her would raise her ugly head again.

As they took stock of their situation they discovered one ship had taken on large amounts of water and would be crippled to the point that most of the cargo and the majority of its crew had to be distributed among the remaining five. They were able to apply an emergency patch to keep her afloat until they reached the port but the feeling was that the ship required extensive repairs and would not be able to continue on. Vice Admiral Horatio expressed that while he was disappointed as the wounded ship was manned by his most experienced office and his closest friend on the voyage. At offices call he explained their situation and commended all on their valiant actions. When he addressed the situation that they would proceed with one less ship all were disappointed yet confident that the mission could continue.

The captain of the battered ship stated with a smile that while he was waiting for repairs he'd have an opportunity to meet his new granddaughter as he arrived in this world and by the time the ship was ready to sail again the harsh winter storms would be over and he could join the other half of the fleet in the spring.

Two days later they arrived at Port Lisbon and started taking on the required provisions. In spite of the storm and the loss of some of the cargo the amount required for replacement was actually less then what at first was expected.

They studied the charts and decided to lay over one additional day as the wind reports from the north indicated that the tumultuous sea was ebbing at unexpected high tides. Vise Admiral Horatio wasn't dissuaded though as he was familiar with the unexpected storms and as he said "You come to expect them."

On one occasion he reflected on an experience he had encountered as a young Lieutenant and stated that things are different now as we have costal reports from all the way on the northern tip of the island including co-operation with the scots.

Although the kings and regents of those northern lands had agreements that were tenuous at best the coastal towns were usually more friendly and open to providing reports as they were able to enjoy some additional trade that increased their commerce.

"Yes sir, it's not like the old days when you never knew what to expect." One of the junior officers overheard one of the senior crew men make the statement that the old slat could bellow enough wind to direct the entire fleet on course. The officer took issue and reprimanded the sailor. He ordered twenty lashes for insubordination. As wais the custom in the navy that all extreme punishments had to be approved by the captain of the ship when the Vise Admiral heard of what was being contemplated he explained to the young officer that the Old Salt agreed with the comment and took it as a complement. When the crew heard the verdict they responded that it's a good thing to have an old salt to put some on the feathers of the shave tail.

After an additional three day delay they were once again headed for the southern tip of the western port of Ireland named Port Murphy. The weather cooperated and the five ships arrived unscathed in only four days. By this time Lady Veronica and her entourage were speaking only Gallic in their conversations and even the Vice Admiral when he spoke to their crew spoke only in Gallic.

"I didn't think I' remember as much as I have since I've not used it in many years but I must say I find it most pleasant." Paul, Trish and the lady in waiting Virginia were pleased to be able to help and always stepped forward to correct any one as they made mistakes. After all a misplaced salable would make the difference between a complementary statement to a person and calling them a son of a dog. Upon arrival at fort Murphy they were met with a less than congenial garrison of the Irish military personnel. Their greetings although cordial enough reflected the tense situation that they found themselves in.

It seemed that with the winter setting in several ships had anchored and fights between the town people and the scurvy crews was harrowing. Some of the taverns along the Warf had been taken over by scoundrels and lawlessness prevailed.

Horatio offered his marines to serve as support to the local law as it was obvious that the town was in disarray. The town leader however turned down his offer. Their reasoning was that while the navy was birth there they would have piece but in a few days when the fleet sailed again the scurvy lawless group would wreak havoc in retribution. The only logical course as the town elders saw I was to allow it to play itself out and once they were all gone life would return to normal.

That being the case Horatio gave the order that anyone of his fleet caught in unacceptable conduct would receive harsh punishment that would be swift and very painful.

Horatio had sent a land crew to skirt the shore around the horn and on the fifth day he received the word he was looking for. The storms on the eastern Ireland side had subsided and he plotted that if they could catch the lee ward side of the currents they could complete their trip around the horn and make it to the next port on their journey in less than seven days if the weather held. They were at the beginning of low tide so he calculated that it would be at least six hours before the new tide started to come in. With any luck they could be deep enough into the sea before they were pushed back towards the shore. Once on the open sea they would be able to make use of the currents and avoid waiting a complete 18 hours before it would be favorable to leave port again as was the custom. Of course one reason people didn't normally do it was that if Mother Nature raised her ugly head during the maneuver it could cost him dearly. As it turned out providence smiled down on his efforts and the storms were delayed long enough to be way out to sea, and as they say the rest is history.

"The Old Salt pulled it off again." As the word spread and the moral of the crew spiked to an all-time high.

They were to need this boost two days hence when they were met with an armada of eleven pirate ships headed by one of the most feared pirate captain along the west coast. While they were no match in a head to head confrontation with the English man of war their ships were faster, sleeker and drew less draft so they could hover in the coves the big ships couldn't enter.

The first attack was fierce as the pirates mistook one of the smaller vessels as vulnerable and launched the attack just as the dawn bean to peek its face across the shoreline. With the sun at their backs they figured they could out maneuver and disable the ship.

What they did not take into account was that Horatio had contemplated this action and held two of the man of war ships with their long range and deadly accuracy to pulverize the three attack vessels. After that the battle continued out as a cat and mouse game. After a week of continued off and on battles the pirate fleet simply disappeared. The score was seven to one and the one damaged British ship could still limp back to port Murphy. The records indicated that the fleet had a minimal loss of life of one junior officer, six marines and four sailors.

A lot of cargo had to be dumped over the side that couldn't be stowed on the other ships but it was necessary to lighten the wounded vessel to insure it would keep afloat while maneuvering back to port. When asked about the sudden break off of hostilities Horatio replied because a new storm was coming our way and hey wouldn't be able to weather it. If it's as large as I looks it might take us under before we can reach our next destination.

He ordered an inventory be taken and only essentials would remain. By dumping a lot of cargo the ship rode high in the water and lessoned the chance of being swamped when the high waves that he knew were to come arrived. At one point they tied the sails completely down, stripped the booms completely off and buttoned down the hatches and prayed that the sea wouldn't drive them on the rocks.

Since Horatio had a command of this area he had ordered the ships far enough out to sea that he figured by the time the storm had spent its fury they would still be far enough out to avoid a confrontation with the rocky shore. As the storm receded and once more they could gain control of their direction he ordered general quarters and battle stations. For the better part of a day and a half they sailed unmolested. Just as some were starting to think the old man had given way to over caution eight black flags arrived on the horizon.

Once again forbearance and meticulous attention to detail saved the day. While many would have been caught off guard the fleet was ready. His plan was to have of his four remaining ships crisscross while firing broad sides at the enemy. Once that was accomplished the two heading straight forward would angle in the same pattern while the original two lined up straight forward once again. This tactic was repeated for four cycles. They broke the back of the black ships as they had counted four ships headed for Davie Jones Locker, another two were crippled badly and the remaining two decided it wasn't worth the expense.

They rallied, retooled the best they could and headed for Port Arbuckle. When they arrived they located a good spot on the lee ward side protected from the winter winds. The fleet commander ordered a detachment of marines to establish an encampment on the upper cliffs to prevent any expected attacks from local marauders and put in for repairs.

They replenished the cargo that they had lost in the storm and set to rearming and repairs. While at bay David (DONALD) and Trish commented that while the ship would take several days to skirt the jut out and a few more to reach their port the journey over land was actually only two to three days away. Lady Veronica relayed this information to the fleet commander and the plans were altered to suit the new development. A contingent of marines could make a bee line for the village they sought and secure it while the fleet would form a blocking barricade to keep the pirates contained. The clock was set into motion and the events that followed were as good a script as could be written.

Clean up proved to be less harrowing than expected as an element of the Irish militia showed up to thwart against the retreat of the pirates into the hills to the north east. The commander of the Irish garrison took charge and thanked the fleet for their involvement. It was the first time in recorded history that the two armies actually fought as allies.

As things wound down and plans were made to return the fleet as it had accomplished its original mission the word was sent that the spring fleet had been delayed due to an invasion from across the English Channel from Spain. War it seemed was the order of the day. Trish and Donald asked to be allowed to stay in their home land and dispensation was granted for Donald as he was released from his obligations of service to the king.

He swore an oath of loyalty that he would forever more work toward the goal of uniting the two nations. Trish had become infatuated with him and they took the marriage vows. Having placed in her mind to always remember them as loyal friends Lady Veronica once more recorded in her parchment that she was looking forward to filing a report with the king and hoped that with the onset of the late spring and early summer she would be allowed to return to her beloved.

She concluded with "How deeply can one express the feelings of love, and say it best. How can one allow to flow, the thoughts that press as on we go. We allow others to see our intent with x's and o's but there is not enough space as emotions grow. The end of the page would not provide even if I filled the other side." With that she placed her lips at the bottom of the page and closed the book.

Chapter 8

"As king of the empire I've got to give way to my private desires and as a member of the court you will have to place your personal wishes on hold." He spoke softly to Lady Veronica and she could see the regret in his eyes and the sorrow in his heart. He had promised her that upon completion of her Ireland mission that he'd move mountains to see to it that she was allowed to continue her quest and rejoin her love.

"I understand your eminence!" You could hear the disappointment in her voice yet it was strong and steady.

"Life often turns on us and we have to deal with it. I shall serve you in which ever capacity that you assign." Her voice lifted a bit and her pride in being selected was evident. She could have thought "It's just not fair" but if she had any such indignations they weren't visible.

"Excellent." He responded, "You must report to Vice Admiral Horatio for your orders." They had been back less than a week and she had just dispatched a letter to Nickolas that she expected to set sail in a few days. As fate would have it, she was to set sail except it was not in the direction that she had anticipated.

So once again she took pen to paper and explained the situation.

"My dearest love, of all the places I'd rather be right now, on a ship to an unknown destination in the service of the king would be my last choice. Yet," she stopped for a few seconds while she gathered her thoughts. "Yet my obligation to serve my king preempts my personal choices and desires. It seems that the forces of evil are determined to keep us apart, but the forces of evil do not know me." The letter continued for some time explaining her activities in Ireland and her content that despite the delay she had found it necessary to close the loop and finish the quest.

Veronica continued to explain how her second trip to Ireland wouldn't have delayed her returning to him as the mission had been completed before the thaws of the northern seas. "The monsters of nature, the wills of mortal men can only hold us apart so long then the strings that bind will break and once more I'll be in your arms." At the conclusion she professed her love for him and how much she was looking forward to being with him once again once this messy situation was completed. She set the seal of the realm on the envelope and entrusted it to her friend and ally The Sea Monster who called her sister. Although her letter wasn't an official dispatch, as a member of the royalty she was privileged to place any letter deemed personal and private with the seal. After that she set out to report to The Vice Admiral.

"Always happy to welcome a trusted accomplice" he said with a grin. "Although on the other hand, considering the circumstances, I wish it didn't have to be." They set sail for Port Irena in the northern province of France as her mission as ambassador was to attain the alliance of the northern French province to establish a port of entry for the British troops and equipment. Although the British fleet was a formidable one there remained the question of just how strong the Spanish Armada was. It simply made good sense to prepare for a ground war if it came to that. Their leverage with the northern French regents was the fact that the Spanish had been raiding their ports for the last year and although they felt they could sustain a ground war they were weak in the naval department. The British could provide protection for the French ports and reinforce the French army to the point that they felt their land would be invulnerable.

Another plus was that the regent of the land where she was heading for was a first cousin and they had been friends since childhood. Speaking French was a plus and with the information that Princes Rhonda had visited the northern land and had obtained some gifts that Nicholas had produced in his shops reinforced her expectations and made her doubly sure that all would go well.

Unknown to Lady Veronica, Princess Rhonda thought that she had suffered a humiliation while on her last trip to the north and held Nicholas personally responsible for the events. Lady Veronica was looking forward to her reunion with her cousin until she received word that she would not be officially welcomed although there meeting would be cordial enough. The Lady was baffled and sent an inquiry pertaining to the matter.

The story retold reflected that the Princess felt she had been slighted by Nicholas. In an attempt to ascertain just what had come to pass she dispatched a note to Nicholas inquiring of the substance of the matter. She scribed a note of apology to the Princess begging her forgiveness for any inconvenience that she may have experienced. Since there was nothing further she could do she resolved to make sure the affairs of state were in order.

Veronica had landed at Irina during a thunder storm and was barely able to dock as the tide reversed and started pulling the ship out to sea again. She was confident though that everything would be okay as she had complete confidence in the ships captains skills. The storm was beating against the dock and extricating her and the remainder of the passengers proved a difficult but not impossible task. After three attempts to unload the cargo they finally just buttoned down the hatches and decided to wait until the storm played itself out. Early the next morning her stuff arrived. Most of it had been soaked during the attempt to off load the day before and had been sent to be dried and pressed. The official documents weren't affected as they had been properly stored and placed in safe keeping.

It was a week before she received any word from Nicholas. He sent his apologies to the princess and offered any reconciliation that he could to right any wrongs. It seemed that the princess had placed an order for her niece about a week prior to her birthday and the word never contained the information that it was a priority order. He further responded that had he known of the rush he would have insured it was completed on time. Since he had already pre commissioned that particular set of toys to be delivered to the orphans of the adjoining area he simply followed normal protocol.

This didn't set well with the princess and she resolved not to deal with Lady Veronica until proper reconciliation and proper contrition was received. Ever the diplomat Lady Veronica simply responded that she would look into the matter however under her breath she thought it was childish. Of course looking back on their childhood, even though she liked her cousin she always thought of her as high strung and a bit selfish.

Of course she could always overlook that as the princess had no younger siblings and always got her way. Lady Veronica decided to overlook the short comings and elected to always put her best foot forward. After all they did share the story of the princess's first kiss and her infatuation with the Prince of the neighboring province.

Later when the Princes discovered he was a prude and the shine wore off his armor she dumped him in a furious argument and the two provinces almost went to war over it. It all settled down when the prince met and fell in love with a lady of a different province and declared that her cousin wasn't worth the effort. That of course resulted in a flurry of messages bouncing off each other until one day the princess found a new pursuit.

Lady Veronica was always reserved and not flirtatious like the princess so when she finally met Nicolas she knew that she knew that it was right.

The proper messages were exchanged and apologies spread out to sooth the wounded pride and protocol was put back in the natural order of things. This ordeal had taken over a month to resolve but in the end as it turned out, it was to the kings' advantage.

He was able to gather his fleet from some of the far reaches and prepare for a frontal assault. The Actual ground preparations were controlled by General Wellington, a proven commander who had led the troops to victory on several occasions. He was most notably known for the Battle of Constantine where his army although vastly outnumbered by three to one managed to pull of a surprise victory. Due to his cunningness he led the enemy into a false sense of security, slipped across the icy river while they were at rest and routed the enemy. The defeat was so devastating for the Hessians that it took years for them to recover.

This time he enjoyed a superior numerical advantage with all of his troops' professional soldiers. When the push began he coordinated with the English bombardment and control of the sea lanes. It wasn't long before the Spanish were giving signs that a parlay was being sought. Since it was the kings' intent to establish predominance on the sea and demonstrate his ability to contain the Spanish army and not to destroy the Spanish aristocracy all together, he was amiable to an honorable peace.

Besides he contended that total defeat of the Spanish would take years as the mountainous terrain would prove them adequate protection and the cost of complete conquest would be devastating to his economy. Besides the Spanish royalty were all second cousins and an overaggressive stand could cause ripples throughout the entire known world. Lady Veronica was happy that she had completed her part if the mission and requested the king release her to pursue her original intent.

"A new home at last." Once again Veronicas thoughts were happy as she looked over the horizon toward the dock. The trip back had been uneventful as the sea calmed and the spring storms seemed to be taking a much needed rest.

The convoy was able to skip the first port as the gentle

southern breeze allowed a direct passage through the straits. It was almost as if God himself had breathed on the sails and lined them up with a arrow point making it possible for maximum speed.

As they arrived at their second point along the travel they were able to dock and obtain all of the replacement provisions required to continue on. The loading went so rapidly that they were actually ready to launch before the tide was favorable. Good weather persisted and they were able to pass the third port. They had made such good time that they were in sight of their final destination within the next three days. As she placed her feet upon the dock once again she could be heard to exclaim "Home at last." ---------------

Her happy thoughts were tainted when she received word that although Nicholas had intended to meet her, duty called. Once again recording the disappointment of the day she jotted a short verse. "It came upon a midnight clear that evil besets myself, my dear, though life may tumble and cause me strife, soon Mrs. Claus I'll be," she paused and concluded "And be your wife." Being well acquainted with the concept she simply arranged for things to be forwarded to the castle. She sent a message that she had arrived and was going to oversee the reconstruction of the castle to insure all was going as planned and returned that evening with a sense of peace she had not known in a very long time. For the next two weeks she was sure to follow her routine of recording all of the events of each day. On one occasion she wrote that the weather had been bad as the rains continued unceasingly and although it was summer now a late winter storm determined not to give way to the new seasons warmth had deposited several inches of snow. While it seemed a bit unusual to her she was assured that such events occurred this far north. While not often and mostly a nuisance, they did occur.

Just as she had resolved to make the best of it she encountered a second situation. For no apparent reason the garrison was attacked. The bandits, it seemed had the mistaken idea that since she was royalty and a Lady of the British Isles that she would be an easy target. They failed to do their homework and were confronted with a Lady with the skills, knowledge and sufficient troops to prepare her position for most every contingency. While the norm was to pull back into one's self during inclement weather Lady Veronica had determined not to allow things that she could not control to cause her to draw back. At the onslaught it seemed that the aggressors had the upper hand as they had a vast numerical superiority. The general wisdom was that it would take a six to one advantage to take a castle and their leaders had calculated that their numerical strength was at least ten to one.

The initial assault was formed to strike fear into the defenders. Their miscalculation cost them dearly as when they massed at the front gate they were greeted with hot oil and a barrage of arrows. After that they attempted the catapults but in order to get the proper position they had to locate in the lower valley. Since the defenders had taken the time to dam the river, once the equipment had been placed and readied for the assault the defenders opened the flood gates and watched the destructions as the weapons floated down into oblivion.

On the second day the sun came up, the weather warmed and the mud bogged down the assault. As the leaders were conferring a contingency of her brother clan arrived. As the two sides had met in battle before the newly arrived clan did not hesitate and pressed forward. Being caught on two sides the aggressors formed a hasty retreat. The last anyone from the castle saw of them they were in a disordered retreat leaving equipment, the dead and wounded strewed throughout the land. After the battle the clan gathered up the remains, collected the dead for the funeral fires and gathered the wounded to serve as slaves. Although Lady Veronica didn't hold with slavery she was a pragmatist and knew the ways of the world.

She recorded all of the events with as much accuracy as possible and was sure to write the names of the chief of the relief clan so she could offer a more formal appreciation in the future. Although she knew that Nicholas was somewhat concerned about her safety, he knew that she'd have it no other way and was up to the task. By the end of the second week they were simply memories written for the records and filed in the archives of history. These records as with most gathered dust for several years. Their memories receded to the back of the mind and it seemed they were destined to go the way of antiquity when at last they were brought back into focus. For now though they just resided between the corners on the rickety old bookshelf in the archives of the library. Five days later Nicholas arrived with one of the first trade trains. He had received a large order and wanted to personally see to it that it was properly shipped. As his name grew other merchants were ordering huge supplies for the Christmas season. Since just in time would not come into being for several centuries merchants were required to be able to determine what was the most likely to increase their profits. Since Nicholas' fame for toys had spread his orders had increased rapidly. He now had three full time factories and was in the process of opening a fourth on at the port of Points-Ville.

The joy of the reunion at the castle was short lived as Nicholas had to continue on with the Caravan. They had taken the evening to simply walk the length and breadth of the castle as she explained to him the plans for renovation. Seeing her anticipations and desires he assured her that in a couple of days, after he had insured delivery of the merchandise that he would return and they would have an entire week together.

Upon arrival at the port Nicholas discovered that due to the wars in the south the merchant ships had been confiscated and transferred into troop carriers. The Spanish, it seemed had determined that they were not going down so easy and were launching an all-out offensive against the British. That being the case he had to make arrangements with several smaller ships. Just as he thought he was all set and making ready to return, one of the ships with his cargo on it limped back into port. They had only been gone two days when they were accosted by a military ship and virtually robbed of all the cargo. All of the provisions had been absconded so they had been left with only enough provisions to return to port. The ships' captain reported that when they discovered part of the cargo was toys from Nicholas they dumped them overboard. After all he was involved with the Lada Veronica of the British Empire.

When he received the report he simply responded "Bad things happen to good people." He immediately dispatched his apologies for the inconvenience and promised replacements to be sent on the next available ship. The entire episode took an additional four days so when he finally arrived back at the castle he was only able to stay for two of the days he had originally planned. "I Sometimes feel that someone is conspiring against us." Nicholas was frowning at the thought that once again circumstances were pulling them apart. Lady Veronica replied "Perhaps, but it won't work. We're stronger than that." Her lips quivered a bit at the thought but she had resolved to be ready at the end of August for the Wedding.

She stroked Nicholas fore head as she whispered "It'll be alright. We'll make it." You could see the stress relief as he relaxed and took her into his arms. "Yes" he replied "It will be alright." His emphasis on the statement gave way to peace and contentment for a short while. They simply sat there holding hands and smiling at each other. "It seems like a long time since we've had an opportunity to just relax. It seems something is always coming up."

She smiled as they stayed for a while lingering in pleasant thoughts. Finally he stated that as much as he'd like to stay the night that he had responsibilities and had to go. They kissed good night and she retired to her room.

That night she was having pleasant dreams about the future her dreams suddenly changed when a fierce dragon swept across the sky breathing fire. The entire room caught fire and the doors were barred shut. When she attempted to advance toward the window scorpions blocked her way and the ceiling fell in.

She abruptly sat up in a pool of sweat gasping for air. It seemed like forever before she was able to draw a deep breath. After she settled down a bit she decided to sit up in the lounge on the veranda. As she scanned the peaceful night stars she wondered what that was all about. She could picture the dragon in her mind as she had seen it long ago as a child. The stories that she had listened to as a young girl came back and the anticipation that she felt resurging combined fear and nostalgia. She had to wonder which side of the scales of good and bad this was on while she attempted to gain control over her emotions. *"Perhaps"* she said to herself *"it's just been brought on by severe stress."* Up to this point in the year things had been moving at a rapid pace and had left her little time to sort it all out. *Now however* she thought to herself *"things will settle down and we can prepare for a wonderful fall."* She just knew that the winter would slow things down and her life would resume at a leisurely pace if that were possible. Eventually her mind drifted back to oblivion and she rested.

Things were not to be that simple though as her nightmare next continued encountering a seven headed snake. At first it seemed passive and indifferent to her presence. As it drew near she could recognize some of the heads as those of former adversaries that she had laid to rest. Each in turn had fallen to her sword, bow and whit. Now however it seemed they had gathered in the underworld and made a pact to bring about her demise. As with most dreams when you awaken you can remember some of the highlights but the details elude you. Once again she woke in a pool of sweat, her nerves were frazzled and their ends were hot and stung like embers off of a roaring fire. She rose and doused herself with the cool water from the wash bowl. With the passage of time she managed to get hold of her faculties as she slowly crossed the floor.

When she looked toward the window she realized that

the dawn was peeking over the mountain so she decided that it was obvious that she had all the rest that she was going to get for that night. She called to see if any of her ladies in waiting were up yet and discovered that they had been aware of her movements throughout the night and as a consequence had been preparing for assistance for several hours. Lady Veronica felt bad about conferring the burden on her maids but of course given her station in life said nothing at the time. Some times its' hard to walk the fine line of leadership and friendship but in true style she weathered the storm.

That morning while having a brief breakfast with Nicholas he informed her that he had received word from his folks that some new crises had occurred. She immediately decided ha she should accompany him but he replied "In our family" with the emphasis on the word our, "a crises arrives twice a week so there is no need to be alarmed." With that information she decided to remain and oversee events. After all it was important to her that she be able to complete all of the preparations as August would be here before you know it.

She had that same gruesome night mare several nights in a row and couldn't shake the feeling that something catastrophic was on the horizon.

Five days after he had departed she received word that a barbaric tribe of some size had gathered and attacked Nicholas while enroot to his town and the fate of the caravan was unknown. She immediately sent messages to her clan to see if she could determine just what had transpired. After a week with no information Lady Veronica decided that sitting tight was not her style and she started making arrangements for exploration. When someone mentioned that if she departed now there was some doubt if preparations would be completed on time for the wedding. She responded that if there was no groom there would be no wedding. Her dreams kept gnawing at her and anticipation mounted as she prepared. Just as she was departing she received word from her brother clan that the force that had conducted the raid was of a formidable size and tracking them would be easy as they left a path of destruction in their wake. Overcoming them in battle though would prove to be another matter. Although her bothers in arms were fearsome warriors in their own right the sheer size of the enemy encampment would be prohibitive.

Chapter 9

As the clans met to determine their potential involvement the conversation was furious and the heated comments went on for what seemed to be forever. While many of the clansmen had looked upon her as an ally some were of the mind that although they owed her an allegiance of sorts they had no responsibility toward Nichols as although he was a nice enough person being nice did not necessarily translate into direct support for rescue. With that in mind Lady Veronica stepped forward and addressed the clan leaders as was her right under the league of tribal law.

Veronica, for her part addressed the council with firm determination. "I have come to obtain information and help if it is forthcoming. I have received the information I need to formulate the rescue of my beloved and I do not hold it in sour if the clan does not decide to provide assistance." The tension was very noticeable and the murmurs among those gathered could be heard almost to the point of becoming a disruption. Lady Veronica paused for a few seconds to allow the discomfort to settle down. "I chose the words (I do not hold it as sour) to illustrate the point that I can live comfortably with your choice if you determine not to support me, yet my course is clear. I shall with or without your help proceed to release my betrothed." With that she bowed politely and receded into the background. Many did not want anything to do with this yet she had some supporters. The final conclusion was that the clans would not officially support her efforts but any individual chief could without retaliation of the collective body assist her if they were foolish enough to do so.

As a result three of the chieftains committed themselves and their clan to assist her. The collective number of warriors tallied some three thousand. Lady Barbara was appreciative of the intent but when speaking to them she cautioned that since their combined numbers were so small when compared to the aggressors that success would depend on total cooperation of all three clans working in unison. The first issue to be addressed then was to have the three chiefs elect a leader who would formulate and coordinate the efforts of all. She was sure to include the fact that she had some three hundred war hardened troops and would subject them to the same standards of the entire group. The three met for the better part of a day and the conclusion was that the chief in charge would be referred to as Regissør the equivalent of the director and his word was to be the law for all to follow. They were well aware of the impossible odds of a frontal attack even though many warriors would prefer to meet their final destination in battle while looking into the eyes of the enemy.

So the die was cast. The plans were drawn and the assignments were made. Quite simply they would conduct a series of attacks on the fringes from different directions causing the enemy to think they were much larger than they were and causing uneasiness within the enemy ranks.

No attempt would be made to rescue Nicholas at any point during the first several days. The goal was to heighten the anxiety of the enemy and keep them guessing at the real goal. Although these were seasoned warriors the only thing that they really had going for them was the fact that the enemy would have to both defend their families and send a formidable force to defeat their enemy. Their attempts to retaliate against the clans attacks were futile as the clans were very familiar with the territory and would simply vanish when the opposition arrived. After three weeks of this type of war they had lost less than fifty men and were quite pleased with their accomplishments.

One evening as they were about to go out for the nightly raid a contingency of an additional fifteen hundred warriors showed up. They had considered the plight of Lady Veronica and had voted to assist. Most of them were well known to the rest and were warmly welcomed. "We figured you'd have this all wrapped up by now." One of the new minor leaders stated. "No" the Regissør replied, "They are a much larger force and although we're successful in what we've achieved so far we are a long way from achieving our goal." The new forces were quickly assimilated into the plan and the attack for the night was modified to include the new forces. The chief of the newly acquired force was quick to mention that it was because of Lady Veronica that he and his families enjoyed the security of life. He Having said that, he reaffirmed his commitment to her with the presentation of a red ribbon. That, as it turns out, is the highest honor one warrior can present to another. In short her cause was his cause.

With the addition of the new segment they were able to expand the plan and the results was that the enemy was, although they thought they were ready, upon their counter attack they were squeezed into the center like a sandwich, sliced down the center and their cost was calculated at over sixty percent of the defending force. That was the result of a suggestion that Lady Veronica made when observing the plans. A quick hit, a vanishing act as had been being used followed by a crushing blow to divide and conquer. While this was going on a small contingent skirted the battle and attacked the village. With most of the warriors on the offensive the camp was relatively unprotected and many families lost loved ones. The results were a devastating blow to an already uneasy awareness that their entire cooperative clan was in jeopardy. With this in mind the leader of the invading force sent a message of inquiry.

"We know that you have something in mind, we know you cannot defeat our forces in battle yet you gnaw at us like a petulance of rats. You cannot defeat us, no we know you. So state your case, just what is it you are swarming like a petulance of flies to achieve." Regissør replied "We have lived our entire lives for many generations in these lands. We have dedicated ourselves to the advancement of our clans and our culture. When you invaded our lands you did so with full intent to destroy our very way of life. Now you have taken what is most valuable to us when you captured an ally who by the way is not a warrior or an aggressor. Our desires are simple, return him and his people to us, keep the goods and supplies that you have acquired and seek to meet us in peace. If you will do this we will stop disrupting your life and you may if you choose reside among us in peace or continue your war like ways and your journey wherever it may take you."

This concept was alien to the chief of the invading army yet he thought he could see some light in this. His captives were, after all mainly useless for this type of life as they were not used to harden manual labor and offered very little to support his clans. With this in mind he offered an arrangement to meet three days hence and return the unwelcome baggage that hung around his neck. Lady Veronica was ecstatic with the news. Up to this time she had worn the combat hunters' uniform playing down her femininity as she wore the badge of honor bestowed upon her for prior battles. This date however, she wished to display all of the grandeur of her position first as a lady then as a representative of a sovereign nation. With all of the regalia and pomp and circumstances that could be mustered to impress the opposition the colors flew in full view. The mild cross wind caused the display to appear even more impressive.

The meeting had been set at a designated place in a valley border on the right side by a torrent river that would delay if not stop any attempts at attack from that side. The left was a series of cliffs where a defensive position was set up just in case. As they observed the advancement of the enemy they readily noted that all were dressed in battle attire with the war horses placed in front. The clan immediately knew that the play for time had given the enemy the ability to muster their full forces to bear down on the assembly. Thankful for her involvement and expe-rience in battle Lady Veronica quickly retreated to the tent where she had prepared for the day.

Striping off the finery of the hooped dresses and re-moving the shining articles from her hair was simple and changing into her battle clothing, strapping the leggings and sliding into her breast plate took no time at all. Having accomplished that, she returned to assume her rightful place at the head of her three hundred marines. She was confident that whatever happened this would be a day to demonstrate the superiority of the civilized world over the barbaric nation beseeching her. The head Regissør did not wait for the charge, he simply ordered the archers to the front to lay a barrage of arrows in an attempt to cause as much chaos as possible. Although they were outnumbered at least seven to one the thought of retreat never entered their minds. "Today is a good day to die" he shouted above the roar of the battle. As was preplanned they backed up some several hundred yards until they were fully within the reach of the walls on the left. The advancing army gave no mind to the walls as they had the idea that the opposition was in full retreat.

In preparation for this event many catapults had been placed on the cliffs and were ranged to pulverize the offensive drive of the opposition. At the start of this phase it seemed the enemy was taken unaware of their position. After all with the superior numbers, no matter how many casualties they sustained the immense weight of their onslaught would result in victory. The three clans formed spear heads to penetrate the onslaught with the hope of driving them into fragmented groups. These could be dealt with in small segments and defeated. Just as the Regissør was about to call for a shift in the position to realign closer to the cliffs for better bow support he saw what at first looked like a splintered portion of the enemy advancing on the high cliffs. It turned out that they had actually preplanned this maneuver and was slowly but surely taking control of the high lands. The battle lasted for several hours and in spite of their valor signs of numerical superiority were starting to show. Most of the defending positions on the high ground seemed to have been lost. Now the only thing left would be for the hordes to thrust a final spear into the heart of the defenders. With all the volume he could muster he gave what he considered his final command. The trumpets were blasted with the sound of the attack and the roar of the defenders went up as they started their charge. All of a sudden the enemy started retreating. There seemed to be no rhyme or reason for it but a pullback was obvious. He didn't give thought to the reason he simply pushed forward taking advantage of his new found strength. In short order it became obvious that relief had arrived. He could see the colors of the many clans flourishing above the cliffs that had been lost and the enemy was being routed. With renewed strength from the sight, in spite of their heavy losses he ordered his men to continue to press forward.

As the last remnant of day light passed into twilight the battle ground to a halt. What had seemed to be a good day to die turned out to be a day of great victory. As the reports came in it was announced that the remaining clans had rethought their position and took heart at the accomplishments of the defenders. When they reassessed the situation they decided that although they owed nothing to Nicholas they were sworn to uphold a recognized member of the warriors of valor and a useless fight against superior numbers actually was the backbone of their society.

The next day they met again with the warring nation. This time it was a different matter. The barbarians had been whipped on the field of battle in spite of their superiority and in accordance with their code they had capitulated to the other side. As the appointed Regissør the chief of the newly organized three clans into one addressed the other side. "You have met us in battle and have lost." The emphasis on the word lost was impassioned to the degree that none could deny the totality of the statement. "However" he continued in spite of your attempt at trickery and deceit we have decided that we do not wish to treat you as a conquered tribe or nation. We simply require you to provide to us that which we came for. First you will" with the emphasis again placed on the word "will," return the captives that you had promised. Second, in spite of your obvious intent to be dishonorable you will replenish our forces and equipment that has been lost in this event. We do not wish to take you as slaves nor do we intend to restrict your departure. Once you have met the requirements you will be free to return to your lands and renew your family ties."

The chief of the opposition stated that he couldn't believe his ears when he heard the demands. They were so preposterously simple that he consulted with his advisors as to the possible intent of trickery that must surely be being planned. It was an unheard of situation where the enemy would be conquered and then turned loose to their own devices to regain their strength. Surely something else must be at play here. They had only been given two hours to comply with the demands and as the time drew near they could fathom no other circumstances where by they would be able to bargain with the others so they simply submitted. Arrangements were made for the immediate release of the prisoners and collections were gathered to replenish the losses of the other side. As far as the idea of restocking the loss warriors they were at a loss as to just what to do about that.

The Regissør sent a party which included Lady Veronica in her full formal dress that no one could take their eyes off of her. She as spokesperson for those she represented presented herself in keeping with the royalty that she reflected and with a dignity unbecoming of a woman of the field. In short they had never seen any woman, even the chiefs wives dressed in their finest, who presented such a magnanimous figure. She spoke softly yet very distinctly. What was even more confusing, she spoke in their language. She left no doubt that she had complete knowledge of the language, customs and nature of their tribes. She explained that although the world is a tough place to live that the existence of nations living in mutual respect was a goal of her king and that if they were willing to stand side by side and serve a common purpose she as the emissary would seal their right to live as an ally.

Details would have to be worked out and each would send representatives to assure the mutual compliance. As for her, she planned to return to her castle and continue her preparations for her wedding. She concluded with an invitation of the former enemy to join her in her celebration of the climax of her life. She knew the road ahead would not be smooth and wide but she was confident that she had been able in the name of humanity and in service to her King to resolve this situation and perhaps make the world a little safer.

Upon return to the castle she found it in disarray. "How can this be?" She asked herself. "I've been gone for only a short while and it seems everything has come apart at the seams." Her inquiries seemed to be fruitless as she could find none of the authorities that she had left to oversee the operation while she was absent. Finally after several hours of searching she found a lower ranking Sherriff hiding in a cellar stuttering and stammering useless sounds of fear and garble. "Get ahold of yourself." She commanded.

"Tell me what the matter is so I can make it right." Although she was somewhat confused and frustrated at what she was looking at she knew she had to take charge and be firm. Eventually the man was able to calm down and start talking again. The story as he related it was the result of a horrible monster that had risen out of the depths of the Boggs and the swamp land to the south. The story met along the lines of the old monster tales that she had heard from the ancient tribes in correlation to that area. A three headed monster, the height of the castle walls with a tail that was as long as the entire side of the edifice. She had a hard time swallowing that story as she knew the peasants had repeated it over the centuries but there was never any proof of its existence. As she surveyed the broken walls she noticed a pattern that resembled the destruction rent by catapults. What stood out were the definite areas of destruction where a direct hit would embolden itself. She thought that although what the frighten defenders saw was definitely a monster she concluded that it was a mechanical monster and the actual destruction was the result of the catapults unseen.

This was a definite setback to her plans yet she determined that in spite of whatever or whoever it was that was intent of disrupting her wedding preparations they would not succeed. Quickly she gathered a small force of fifty soldiers to scorer the southern region while she continued her renovations. She gave explicit instructions for the searchers that they were not to engage the enemy but simply record their activities. She was sure that the force, whatever it was would be immensely larger than her scouting force and a battle would be fruitless and result in an unacceptable loss of life. Although she knew that her marines were fearless and would fight to the last one standing fell she also cared for her supporters and warned them to be careful. She placed a young lieutenant in charge of the party. She selected him as she had seen him in action and was confident that he would not charge headlong into an unwinnable situation.

Three days later the lieutenant reported back and it was exactly as she expected. Some of the local tribes had gathered together to exploit the ruse that the monster had returned. It seemed that in spite of her attempts to insure that the locals were cared for they did not trust her. The stories that her king was intent on expanding his territory to include their homes, along with the tales of his cruelty to those who opposed him were prevalent and they wanted nothing to do with being his subjects.

In her usual fashion of humility and grandeur she organized an Ent rouge to visit the villages in question. Her message was entirely that she was completely enthralled with their country as it was and she had absolutely no intention to making any changes. Her usual appeal was to the chiefs and the mayors of each village. She would start with the acknowledgement that they were wise leaders who cared so much for their people that they were able to form them into a cohesive entity to protect the entire region. She made it known that although she was from a kingdom where her ruler was supreme that he had no interest in developing or conquering this area. She did leave open the option of trade as she always was sure to mention their works of art and other artifacts that were intriguing to her countrymen. In short order she was able to win over at least a situation of neutrality and always concluded with an invitation to her wedding. Satisfied that she had pacified the situation she returned to continue her unfinished business.

Chapter 10

As it happened the humans, as creatures of this earth created a Dimi god who was identified as a three headed serpent who breathed fire and swung a three pronged tail at least as long as its body. They had named him Hydra and determined that this fearsome creature would grow two additional heads each time one was severed. Since the porthole was located in the southern region in the swamp land and far from any human entities the serpent slipped through the opening with the intent to subjugate all of the humans. His terror reigned throughout the region and after the humans had decided that he was actually a hindrance to their continued existence they determined that they should find a way to defeat this dragon. After years of attempting to destroy it they decided that they would require help so they formed an alliance with some of the tribes of the north. One such tribe was the Keno with whom Lady Veronica had made an alliance as she had gained respect of her former adversary. So they sought her assistance.

As a Christian and a follower of Jesus she in turn went in prayer to the one true God as she knew him to be. When God realized that the creature had slipped through the porthole he decided that he would help get him back into the other realm but he would only help and not do all the work himself. *"After all"* he mused, *"They brought it into existence and they should be the ones who contain him. Since this is a world of idols that they made on their own and decided not to believe that only I can transform energy to matter, as a matter of belief they should be able to take care of it themselves."* This situation carried on for many years well into a second generation. The humans of that region were terrified and those who heard of it were at a loss to know what to do. Once the petition was presented to Lady Veronica she agreed to look into it. At first she was suspicious of these tails as she had encountered them before when the locals had tried to scare away her and her party. With a lot of skepticism she decided that she would look into the matter. On the other hand she knew that God works in mysterious ways and such a creature could exist if He willed it. With that in mind she sent for any records, historical and imagined to become acquainted with her adversary.

She found it uncanny that this beast should so closely resemble the Greek beast that the hero Hercules had defeated centuries before. She studied up on that folk lore and after several months of research and consultation with the official church she determined that the creature did in fact exist and needed to be returned to his realm. Of course she knew nothing of a parallel universe so her intent was to send him into the abyss. She was sure that she could not kill the creature as long as the humans who had brought him into existence still believed in him so destruction was the last thing on her mind. In order to get a handle on this situation she sent several scouting parties

out, again with the instructions not to engage this unknown creature but to gather as much information about
it as she could.

What she was able to determine was that for some
reason it had a tendency to stay in a particular area and
never actually ventured outside that area unless provoked
and then only for short periods of time. Identifying his
range and his habitual return to a specific geographic
location she determined that perhaps it became useless
as far as a destructive being when it was gone from its
home base for an excessive period of time. The second
thing she did was to take provocative actions against it at
the very edges of his domain and see how far she could
entice him to wander from his base. The idea was that if
she could lure him out of his environment for some periods of time that she could set up a trap whereby he'd be
unable to break free. Once she accomplished this she
thought she'd be able to determine a way to force him
back into oblivion.

All the while I Am was watching and determined to
himself that he had made the right decision when he had
created her with special abilities for longevity as a help
mate to Nicholas. Through a series of cunning incursions
she was able to draw the creature further and further from
its domain. On each occasion she noted that his strength
was reduced significantly and there would come a point
where she would be able to capture it, sedate it sufficiently
to enable her to return it to its center point and hopefully
pass him through the abyss. It took some time to locate
the area that she knew must exist and had identified in her
mind as a black hole. Once that point was discovered she
concentrated on drawing the creature further and further

away from its lair. Each time, while she had it distracted and away from its home base she would send in a team to construct a pulley system where she could raise the creature over the center of the hole and once centered she could dump him by releasing the net that he was held in.

Since she couldn't determine the depth of the hole she assumed it went to the center of the earth. According to the information she was able to obtain the creature couldn't fly so once it was released into the abyss tons or rock could be dumped into the hole and perhaps fill it so the beast couldn't get out again. Once again she wasn't looking to kill it as she kept in the back of her mind that although Hercules had been credited with its destruction apparently it still lived. She had in the back of her mind that one day perhaps it would find a way to be released again, but then as far as she was concerned that would be for another hero to contend with.

At one point she decided that she had laid the ultimate plan and would be able to capture the creature. One thing that worried her was its ability to breathe fire. Surely any ropes she could devise would burn and it would continually escape. In order to offset this she studied the situation carefully and determined that the blat of the sheep distracted the beast whenever it was ravishing about. So the plan as she laid it out was to entice the beast with the sheep. She wanted to have a sufficient number to entice him further and further from the center. The plan was to ensnare it into a net and then release one or more of the sheep to distract it. The result was that it would release fire to burn the rope net and then use fire again to burn the sheep. Lady Veronica determined that through a series of irritations she could draw it further and further from its lair. Each time once the experiment was completed the beast would return to its home base. The odd thing that they noticed was that it didn't notice the changes made, the structure that was being constructed or the piles of rock and boulders that were being brought in. They didn't know if it noticed the changes or if it did and just discarded them as something not worthy of its time and effort to do anything about. One day while in consultation with some of the knightsof the round table she was informed of a new net that was constructed out of chains of steel. While it wouldn't last forever it should be sufficient to capture the beast especially if it had used a lot of its reserve gasses.

With that in mind she set up for the final encounter. The beast did not seem to notice its diminished powers whenever it ventured outside of its realm. The thought pattern was that it was either unaware of its diminished capabilities or it didn't care as it figured it could always return to its lair to recharge. In either case it worked in Veronica's favor and she was able to entice the creature outside its realm, cause it to expel several fire balls, hopefully enough to weaken him when the final trap was sprung, and contain him within the net. It worked with a few flaws and some of the marines were severely burned but not so that they couldn't recover in time.

The final battle was fought in a valley where she had sheep dispersed surrounding the creature causing it the go into a frenzy and start shooting fire in every direction at once. After several hours of this diversionary action she was confident that the creature would be sufficiently depleted of its ability to spew fire balls at will so she lure it into an area where she had several sheep congregated. The steel net was placed in such a fashion so as to be dropped over the serpent when it was at its weakest. She was quite surprised at its resilience and the number of sheep that it was able to devour before it was finally contained. They had devised a path with a series of buckets of water that they continually poured over the beast while they had it in tow. As it turned out the water idea although it helped turned out to be the worse of the situation as the beast would breath fire even in its weaken state and the water would be turned to steam. This resulted in several of the marines on her mission to suffer burns.

When she finally got it back to the abyss she decided that it would be cruel to dump it into the abyss while still chained so she had constructed the pulley to swing and hung it over the center over the black hole. At the last minute she released the changes and it tumbled into the hole. Everyone held their breath while they waited to see if it would be able to return. After several minutes they could feel the earth quake and decided that a speedy hasty departure was the proper action to take. Once the ground settled with several aftershocks, they revisited the site only to find that the solid boulders had fallen into the crevice and it gave no signs that a hole had previously existed. Once accomplished, she decided that she had encountered enough excitement for this area and reported back to the locals that she had completed her mission. Once again I Am congratulated himself on his wisdom in selecting her for Nicholas's mate. Veronica not aware of the I Am plan was content to return to her new home at the castle and finish her plans for her wedding day.

Chapter 11

Once again Lady Veronica met with the unexpected. She spent most of the past two weeks overseeing the renovations of the castle. Her special day was just around the corner and she wondered if she would ever be able to get everything done on time. "Not to worry, my lady" her oldest and dearest lady in waiting Barbra consoled her, "With all of us working together we'll be ready." Her voice had a soothing quality and her confidence expressed such a whimsical fashion that it was a constant reassurance that surely all would be well. "Yes, I know" Veronica stated after a few seconds of contemplation, "Yet" she hesitated again "Yet I can't help but think that I've left something out." Barbra simply smiled with that fresh look that came across her face whenever doubt came into Veronicas mind. "Surely you'll not fret over some minor obstacle on your special day. Once it has arrived you'll put it in the back of your mind and simply enjoy the moment." Once again her ability to reassure her lady and her seeming ability to float about as she moved with grace set Veronica at ease.

With less than a week to go Nicholas arrived to insure his part in the event was set up to go smoothly. He related to her how he had managed to get things back on track and get the system moving again. They spent the next several days going over the particulars and rehearsing things down to a tee. Late in the afternoon of the day before the great event was to happen Nicholas came to Veronica with a quizzical message. She could tell by his manor that he was uncomfortable and very unlike him he was having difficulty in saying just what was on his mind.

"Veronica" he started, boldly at first, then his voice tapered off and his eyebrows seemed to droop. At first she just looked at him astonished. This was so unlike him that she could imagine all sorts of terrible things. Perhaps he was having second thoughts, perhaps he had a love of the past that he had never gotten over and couldn't go through with this. She was at a complete loss as to what was to come next. Her world was falling apart at the seams and she had no way to control it.

"Surely" she told herself "Whatever it is we can work this out." She took in a deep breath, reached out her hands and with a quivering voice replied "What is it my love?"

"Veronica" he started again "I have something to tell you and I don't know how to go about it." Once again shivers went up and down her spine. "Surely we can work it out, whatever it is." She thought once again. She stepped closer, placed her hands upon his cheeks and whispered "Whatever it is, we can overcome it." She was trying to place a smile on her face as a reassuring gesture yet her insides felt that they were exploding. "What in the world could possibly be wrong? How could this come about in such a short order and where would it lead next."

"NO" he replied with a shout, "I'll not let this come

between us, I've got to tell you." He stopped for a breath and she simply stood there in a statue form unable to move. Her eyes were darting across his face as every-thing else lost its focus and she just couldn't imagine what was going to happen next. Once again he started, this time in a more subtle tone. Considering the dreams that she had experienced recently her insides completely stopped. Her heart quit beating and she was unable to move a mussel.

"I've got to tell you of a dream I had the other night. It has come back to me over the years that I never under-stood. I never put a lot of stock into it as humans always have dreams and sometimes they are repeated many times. My dream, although a pleasant one, has come to haunt me over the past few days. I've always dreamt that I would live a long, long time and I've always taken comfort in it as I always thought of all the good I could do. Now I've fallen in love with you and the thought of living a long time scares me. I'll be here and one day you will grow old and I'll lose you to time. His eyes searched hers as he gently touched her face.

"What a wonderful man you are." She responded. Her heart went soaring towards the sky and her worries were all dispelled into a mist. "What a wonder marvelous beautiful man you are. So now I have a confession of my own. I have had similar dreams over the past years but I never knew how to put them into view. They never really made sense until now. You see," she stopped to take a breath "I've been worried about the same thing. I've always known that for some reason I was destine to live a long while and always looked forward to it. Once I determined that I was to become your wife I placed those thoughts aside hoping to resolve them in the years to come. In the mean time I determined that I was going to accept my place in this world and do everything I could to insure I did the right thing by our God and place my trust in him to resolve the problem.

"This, this is the big problem that you had? This is what was causing you to worry so much. This, the thought of living your life without me after many years together was the sore spot that blemished our lives? No my love it will not be a hindrance to our lives. We'll face whatever comes together and we'll always be here for one another." With that she danced around the patio and swung her arms into the air with grace and a positive attitude. "Yes" she repeated again "Nothing will deter our love as long as we have each other." All of the burdens that had weighed so heavily on her were lifted and she could not fathom anything better. Her life was being wrapped up in a single commitment on the morrow and she and he would spend a life time together. Nicholas felt much relieved that he had addressed this issue with her and now had it in his mind that his dreams although they were so elusive would all patch together and they were destined for a life time of joy and peace.

She rose early the next morning scurrying around attempting to take care of last minute details. Barbra calmed her in her usual methodical fashion as she helped the Lady prepare for the big moment. "After all" she reminded Veronica, "you only have to go through this once. That will be the joys part. That's where the real work begins." She smiled at Veronica and placed her hands upon her shoulders. Barbra had always been close to her and had always had that motherly manor that caused the lady to calm down and face whatever was to come with a grin. "Only beautiful thoughts today." Barbra continued "Only the thought that come what may you will face them as partners and nothing can come in your way." With that Lady Veronica decided that whatever was to be would be and anything that stood in her way would be overcome as happiness was the order of the day.

As she entered the great hall and proceeded down the aisle she put all thoughts of any deviance out of her head. She was going to concentrate on placing one foot in front of another in a cadence that she had practiced several times. Enough times that it seemed to be a natural walk. She tunneled her vision on the priest at the alter and never for a minute had any doubt that she was there on that day to complete one phase of her life and open a new chapter. All of a sudden she had butterflies throughout her stomach. Her legs felt like wobbly sticks of cooked spaghetti and her focus diminished to a blur of confusion. At that point she felt an arm shore her up and she could see the face of the king. He was standing beside her and had a steady grip. *"Surely this can't be?"* she quizzed herself, *"If the king were here, I'd know of it. How could this possibly be that he could arrive and I'd not know of it?"* Yet there he stood in all his grandeur and she could feel that he was real.

"Your majesty?" her voice trembled with a combination of fear and happiness.

"Yes my lady?" He responded "It's been quite a problem keeping this a secret. Yet nothing brings me more joy than to walk you down the aisle and present you to your betroved. I'll explain it later." They took several more steps then Nicholas, in all his grandeur stepped forward, took her arm and stated "Thank you my lord, I'll take it from here." The actual exchanging of the vows only took a few minutes but in her state of mind it was the most memorable time of her life. They exchanged their prepared statements that they had rehearsed so many times that she didn't have to think about how they would sound. She knew and she knew that he knew. After the exchanging of the rings they turned down the aisle and started their new walk as man and wife.

Once the procession was over they met in the great meeting hall with all their friends and allies. Lady Veronica had been sure to invite all the chiefs of all the clans and their families. The town's folks came from miles around to celebrate this happy occasion and even a contingency from the far southern marsh lands had been sent in a token of allegiance and alliance. She had the occasion to speak with the king and he explained how difficult it had been to keep it all a secret. After all the king of all of England couldn't simply board a ship and go on a leisure cruse without extensive preparations. Since the trip was to be done in total secrecy a ruse had to be set up to keep a continual stream of information about his whereabouts and his routine to keep anyone off guard who might have ill intentions for him. Going about a trip with all the usual fanfare and security wasn't an issue until it became a secret. Yet on the other hand he had determined that only God would stop him on this quest. So after many weeks of deceptive preparations he was able to pull it off. He said that he would stay for another few days but that his duties required for him to leave and although he'd had a wonderful time and was ecstatic about his part in the operation his duties called and he wouldn't be able to stay as long as he wished. Lady Veronica thanked him with all her heart and said she understood. Only once before, had it been recorded that the king of any nation had been able to pull this off. It was so long ago and distant in memory that to most it was just folk lore. It was said that over a thousand years prior the King of Prussia had accomplished such a feat and that the expense was so great that it almost bankrupted his entire country.

The celebration went on continuously for six days. On the morning of the seventh Nicholas announced that although he was not a king of an empire he had obligations to attend to and that he and Veronica were departing for a secluded spot unknown to most in order to make preparations for their new life. Veronica had known that their time in what they referred to as eternal bliss would actually give way to the realities of life, yet when that day came she marked it as the end of one life and the beginning of another. Now she had accepted an obligation to be a partner in Nicholas' life and was to go wherever he was to lead. She stored the memories of this transitional day and placed them in her book of memories to be recalled in quiet moments as the years passed by. Actually while she knew that this time would come, she never gave it serious contemplation as an immediate issue, but now the time had come and life was to move on.

Since they had spoken of the issue of longevity and their role in life he had never spoken in as blunt of terms as he now relayed to her. He told her of a visit he had with an angel and a set of instructions that he had been given. He stated that he was quite surprised at what had been revealed to him and although he always knew he had a mission he never had a clear meaning as to what it meant until his visit on the prior night. "First" he indicated with his hand "we are to leave this place and relocate in another country far to the north. "Second, we will be required to sever all our relationships with our current friends and alliances." This took her back a bit as she never thought of resigning from the world in order to in effect establish a new one. "But what of our commitments hear and back in my home country of England?" She wasn't rebellious or irritated at the thought; she simply didn't understand how this was all going to work. "Well" he continued "The angel of the Lord told me that a way would be provided and all that we have gathered here in this life would be passed on to the next generation. They will have found memories of our passing and one day in the far, far future we will be remembered as the ones who established a way for all to remember the Lord Jesus Christ. I'm not sure how that will all work out, but I've been instructed to follow my assignment and leave the worry up to Him. So we've been given thirty days to realign our lives and start our journey. With that they knelt, held each other's hands and prayed a simple prayer. "Oh Lord" they started in unison "allow us to know what you have in store for us and provide us the wisdom to carry it out."

"Well" she concluded I'll have to set things in order properly so I'll need to inform the king of our new mission in life and resign my title as Lady. The servants will need to be released and returned and the marines will have to be sent back in the service of their king. The first thing that she did was to call her immediate entourage of servants and the captain of her marine guard. She explained to them as much as she understood and that they would be returned to the service of their king as she would no longer be a charge of her old country. "It's all so confusing" she stated "but although I will no longer be a Lady in the service of an earthly king I will be a servant of our eternal one."

Barbra at once took up the banner and stated that since she was no longer a lady of the court of England that she, Barbra was no longer obligated to serve Veronica as she did for so many years. With tears in her eyes she extended her hand to Veronica and requested that now that she was no longer under the obligation of serving her, could she accompany her as a friend. Veronica pulled her close and embraced her as tears welled up in her eyes. "I have always considered you as a friend and now we can be so without the pretense of a station in life interfering with our friendship. Of course I want you as a friend."

The next hurdle was to inform the marines. Many had been with her a long time and a couple had been in her service that she could not remember a time when they were not there. Her captain of her escort, O'Malley, had relayed to her on one occasion that his first assignment was when she was on a trip to a castle in the north region when she was only four years old. He had been with her ever since and couldn't fathom what it would be like not being in her service. They had become good friends over the years and she had confided in him on several occasions just as if he were her equal. She always thought of him as a fatherly figure and held his council close. Although he was no longer the young dashing figure of a warrior that we all reflect upon ourselves to be and his beard had grown longer as the years passed with white peeking around the edges he remained in her eyes a place of rest when the world came crashing down around her. Her earliest remembrance of him was wondering how an Irishman ever came to be a captain in the service of the English King.

After all can you trust an Irishman? That phrase was with her as long as she could remember but she never knew why. Captain O'Malley inquired as to the possibility that he could remain in her service as he had always considered her family and he was quite sure several of the marines in her service would feel the same. She said that she didn't think it would be possible as they were first and foremost in service to the king and sworn their allegiance to him for life. As was the custom, once assigned and successfully completing a mission as a guard of a royal person most marines remained in that service for the remainder of their active life. A few had married back at home and had a desire to return to their families whenever the chance presented itself. Some had married over the years to a local girl and they traveled as best they could as a family. All of those who were married or had a sweetheart locally wanted to remain so they ask to be included in the list of those who would be allowed to be in her service even though she would no longer have a formal station in life. With so many formal requests she decided that she would appeal to the king and stated that although they had been most loyal in their service she had befriended them and wondered if something couldn't be worked out.

When she was speaking to Nicholas about it he paused for a short while, sat as he drank his tea and finally said that even though he knew of her close attachments that their services would have to be terminated. "After all" he contended "in spite of our desires and feelings we need to be practical. As I told you I have been told that we will live long lives and be separated from those we now know and love. It's just not possible. You'll have to tell them that although you are deeply touched your station in life has been changed and you must now submit to the services of your husband and your heavenly king. No!" She could detect the sadness in his voice and she came to realize that he also had this issue to contend with. "No, it just won't work." He stated again. Veronica pulled in her belt buckle, swallowed her pride and returned to the marines. "We have had quite a life together and I'll always remember you, each and every one, fondly. However what we wish to be is not possible. You are to return to your stations and accept whatever new life is before you and I must do the same." Barbra looked into her sad eyes and they wept as they held each other for the last time. "Yet, I will always be your friend and if you need me I'll do whatever I can to be there for you." Barbra stated as she packed the last of her belongings. "If we never meet again this side of heaven I'll be waiting for you on the other side." Once again the tears flowed as they hugged their last good bye.

Chapter 12

The shift in their lives had been quite an experience. Nicholas and Veronica always knew that they were to have a special life together and that one day they would be able to look back on it and say with confidence "We've done good." As for now though, they had to contend with life as it was dealt out. As it turned out a transition from the knowledge of being a mortal with a certain amount of time on this earth to entering the realm of the unknown due to an extended life cycle, although exciting was tumultuous at times. What they discovered was that the I Am had created a special place in a parallel universe for them. It had a port hole at the north pole of the earth and its location would always remain a secret to the inhabitance of this world. Since humans had no point of reference where they could point a finger and state that a special area existed somewhere around the north pole where a famous couple lived they had no idea of how or where they came from or to whence they went when they suddenly disappeared.

The actual transition took place over a period of years. She reluctantly left their castle that she had so meticulously planned and processed for their future. The reconstruction of the walls the new window views over the valley below and her plans of serving first her God, then her husband and finally her king. She knew that a relationship had been formed and once she realized the extent of her new life she resigned herself to say good bye and sever her ties with the English Crown. Somehow it seemed that the king had always known that whatever they had in a prior life, it was not to continue so he responded "Greetings my Ex-Lady Veronica. I don't know how but I always knew that your position in life was not relegated to subjugation to my realm. Just recently I had a dream about you where you vaporized from this earth and adjoined with Nicholas in what can only be described as a nonadjacent land. One, although it exists, is nowhere to be found on this earth. From what I gathered you and your beloved are now subject to a higher calling and perhaps we'll never meet again on this earth but I'll see you at heavens gates. Although I understand your desire to excel in your new life I don't think I'll ever understand its true meaning while on this earth. I suppose the only sorrow is in knowing that those who love you so dearly can't be with you. I'm sure one day the Lord will explain it all and we'll gather around that great table enjoying out part in his victory." That was the last communique she ever received from him. Some years later she was informed that he, as everyone else in this world of temporary existence had completed his time on earth and had been laid to rest next to the tombs of his fathers.

As they approached the area identified as the North Pole they found that contrary to belief it was not a cold desolate forbidden place where nothing but ice crystals grew. They, with a small select group had braved the unknown and headed north as instructed. Since they had been on the road, so to speak, for some weeks she began to wonder if they were ever to arrive or if they would simply go so far north that they would be headed south again on the other side of the world. Nicholas remained confident in their course and maintained that the progress each day was coming closer to its end. They had descended into a verboten looking valley where the mist had become so thick that their progress was slowed almost to a crawl. She had wondered if at some point they might simply step off a cravat and into the darkness of eternity. Nicholas would have none of it though and they continued on their journey.

All at once the sky's cleared and before them stood the mouth of a huge cave. She couldn't see the top or the breath of it but knew somehow that they had arrived. As they entered the sense of passing through into another life was a feeling that they all encountered. "Did we die and go to heaven" one of the travelers queried. "I don't think so" Nicholas responded "I believe this is where we are to set up our new homes and the entrance to and from the cave will be our connection to the earth. It's almost like we're in a different dimension." They found the climate quite to their liking and it seemed that each member instinctively knew where they should establish their residence. It was just a matter of a few days and they had laid out the plans for their living quarters and the map of the new township. There was a lot of work to be done but the food was always plentiful and to the liking of each individual. The ale ranged from simple water to refined distilled liquid and each in turn found it to their liking. They didn't know the width and the breath of it but the more space they required the more they found that it was available.

Nicholas headed up a scouting party to map the lay of the land. He soon discovered the answer to the questions about obtaining plenty of lumber for their homes and the toy factories he had in mind. When they left their old home country there were plenty of trees but as they progressed into the north they became scares and further apart. The last couple of month's they hadn't seen even one tree and he was beginning to wonder just how this would all work out. After all his entire world was reliant on trees to provide shelter warmth and materials to build homes and his toy factories. They had been traveling for about a week when they crested a hill. They observed the first trees. They could see three distinct valleys and each one was covered as far as the eye could see. The first, on the extreme right teemed with oak, the center valley was interspersed with hickory and spruce and the valley on the left was completely covered with pine.

He pulled out his eye glass which was powered to 50 and after a cursory glance proclaimed that he could see no end to the forests. What's more, it seemed the climate had changed and they no longer required heavy bulky clothing for warmth. "It almost as if it was made in heaven." One of the explorers stated in awe. "It was." Nicholas simply replied as they scanned the entire country side. He organized a team to start the harvest and assigned another team to go back and obtain horses and wagons to transport the lumber back to the saw mills.

With the first load they formed a station and started the wagon chain. His newly formed civilization consisted of twelve districts each with 144 men. Each district was named after the twelve tribes of Israel as it was Nicholas intent to insure that everyone was constantly reminded of the fact that we are all God's creatures and always subject to His will. Many of them had brought families and the younger unmarried ones lived in lumber camps established for their comfort. Nicholas hadn't planned it that way but simply accepted it as it developed during the process of selection. He was aware that he didn't have all the answers but knew without reservation that God was in total control. Each of the 12 provinces had a sufficient number of hunters and scouts that they were able to track the migration habits of the herds. In almost no time at all they were established with plentiful game to meet their needs. One thing that they discovered was that the deer were able to cover immense amounts of ground with a single leap.

So while everything seemed to be coming up roses the unexpected happened. The territory between their selected home base and the forest that they had happened upon was steep jagged solid rock. Nicholas had never seen granite before and had to carefully scrutinize it to determine its hardness content. Their current picks and shovels were not sufficient to break other than the crust so the initial attempt to create a way through and pave the assent in steps proved to be an arduous task that seemed unsurmountable. He thought surely with enough people working long hours into the night they would be able to overcome the problem. The project suffered set back after set back while many of the workers were injured. One source of the injury was the sudden unannounced breaks in the foundation. It would go from solid granite to shifting sand almost in a heartbeat and swallowed several of the beast of burden and a few of the men. This loss had never entered into Nicholas's mind and he was emotionally devastated when it happened. He was a personal friend of one of the first to be caught up in the quick sand slide that caused a drop of several hundred feet. He sent out inquires among his people in an attempt to gain a handle on how to overcome this phenomena but all were stumped. Then at one point they came across a small boy who had been orphaned before they left their homeland and he offered a possible solution. While it seemed that there was no rhyme or reason to this structure the boy noticed that the variance between the granite and the sand was consistent. While it would be all but impossible to cut through the granite and then bridge the sand it would be reasonable to cut small passage ways through the granite at various locations and then allow the sand to carry the lumber to the bottom to the next crevasse then tunnel through the granite to the next sand base. What they discovered was while the forest was protected by the surrounding mountains slides could be built alternating from rock to sand and provide a way to the base camp below where the wagons could be loaded.

After they had worked on that for a while someone discovered a method of heating the sand and the rock which crystalized and formed a substance they called obsidian. Since it could be cut and forged into tools it was by far a better tool than anyone had ever encountered. So the bellows were created and the burning heat served to solidify the sand. After several try's they were able to use the Obsidian and direct the flow of the shuts. Once that was accomplished they were able to go back to what they knew how to do best: cut down trees and make useable lumber of it.

After several weeks of hard labor and disappointments

Nicholas called for a celebration. Everyone had been working very hard and time had passed without notice. One of the men stated that he was glad that Nicholas had finally come to his senses and enabled the men to get back to their families. Upon arrival at the home base they found that several improvements had been made in their absences. For one thing a saw mill had been completed, most of the homes at least had frames and a few actually had complete walls and ceilings. Upon making an inquiry the men discovered that the women had gathered together as a unit and decided that they would not wait on the men to come back. They proved resourceful and ingenious in their construction and with few exceptions had things ready for the men when they arrived. Some of the younger boys, those not yet old enough to be used on the lumber milling and hauling had stayed back and started construction on the first toy factory. They even had some toys made, enough to justify giving out gifts to the people in their old home land.

While Nicholas had been away a few of the younger children, both boy and girl were able to befriend the local animals, especially the deer. As they gained the trust of the animals they were able to harness them and use them to pull loads that were seemingly much greater than the horses that they had brought with them. The cold didn't seem to bother them or slow them down like it did the horses and they proved much more efficient at pulling the weight. One puzzling aspect of this was that the more you stacked on them the heavier you made the load, the longer and wider you made the wagon they were to pull never seemed to phase them and it seemed they actually grew stronger.

Children, being naïve didn't let what grownups knew about the laws of physics deter them. They simply accepted the fact that they had a friend who would do as they ask. They were able to accomplish what adults simply knew to be impossible. Using these abilities they would load enormous amounts of product to their sleds and direct the deer to the location that they wanted them to go. In many cases this would be accomplished in a single bound. A member of the district of Naptali commented that if this could be duplicated in the world outside this realm it would be most useful for getting around. He envisioned using the deer to replace the ships that hauled the cargo around the globe. He was reticuled by some of the members of Zebulon who stated that in spite of his apparent wisdom he didn't take into account that the deer would leaps so far so as to jump clean off the side of the earth. Others, while they kept their council to themselves simply smiled at the thought of two groups attempting to outdo each other in the story telling realm.

"Well" Veronica stated "I was beginning to think that we'd have to come find you in order to celebrate our first Christmas together." "Actually" he responded "I had lost all sense of time and we only stopped to gather our thoughts and lay out the new plans." "So?" she responded with a devious smile "You'd prefer your lumber over a hot cup of cholate and a occasional snuggle." She giggled and turned to her chores. "Not on your life." He responded. "This is one time I'm actually glad that we needed a break." He reached over and gently pulled her to him. "Perhaps we can take some time off and just enjoy each other as we celebrate the Christmas season. She snuggled up closer in his arms and quietly replied "That would be nice."

Chapter 13

Nicholas was reflecting on the past and stated "Up to this point we've been concentrating on how much we will accomplish during our life. Now we have to decide exactly where we're going and how we're going to expect to get there."

While it seemed that many waters had passed under the bridge of life it had become apparent to him that without verbalization of their quest put into a sequential context all that they had accomplished over the past several hundred years would wind up without meaning. He wanted to get it down in as much detail as he could to insure that the real meaning for their existence wasn't lost in the wrappings of celebration and the presentation of gifts.

He decided to start with Joshua his latest son born some fifty five years ago and now residing in the new found country of America. Joshua had met Martha and together they had carved out a life in the new country and celebrated the birth of Jesus every year for the past twenty seven years. They stuck together during the Great War for independence and had four sons who all were lost during the conflict and two daughters. Both daughters had married soldiers and both husbands returned although one, Emmerit, married to his older daughter Malesia had been severely wounded. Emmerit lost a leg due to wounds and gang green that had set in, but he never lost his faith in God and later in life went on to be a representative of the people. Hastings who had married to the younger daughter Eileen returned to his small farm and worked as a black smith. They had seven children and although they lived a simple life they too had faith in God and remained faithful to him.

Nicholas remembered speaking to Joshua during one of those times right after getting notice that he had lost three sons in the same battle. It seemed for a time that Joshua had given up hope and there would be no Christmas that year as the date for the battle was the seventeenth day of December and they were all looking to a Christmas together as his sons were all stationed so close and it seemed the enemy was going to stand down for the holidays. Of course there was no happy holiday that year but in spite of his apparent bitterness towards God he respected the wishes of his wife and they sat at the dinner table with the three plates turned down.

Later while speaking to his father Joshua related that although his h Martha reminded him of who he was and why hope was the only way to react in this situation. While telling Nicholas about it he broke into quiet sobs and was asking forgiveness for shaking his fist at God and stating that he was so grieved that he could never speak to him again. Yet after a time he came to realize that Martha and his other children were right and that you can't presume to judge the ways of God. "It still hurts dad but now I am able to grasp hold of the real meaning of Christmas and realize the pain and suffering He must have gone through when we crucified his son."

Nicholas remembered trying to comfort his son yet he had experienced the same doubts over the centuries. He and Veronica had birthed three hundred and seventy seven children, had over a thousand grandchildren and no telling how many from the generations that followed. They had all of the photos in the great display hall and he often would spend some time there. Mostly he was accompanied by his wife but on a few occasions he would slip into that area just to reflect. It was on one of these moments that he had decided that it was important that the record be set straight so that someday everyone would know and be able to recognize his reason for being.

When he approached Veronica with the idea he was pleased to find out that she, without making a big deal of it over the years had kept notes and letters about and from all of the children. When she took him to the storage house he found several rooms packed with chest that had the names of all of the children. Within those walls she had kept following generations and their exploits. Nicholas was amazed at amount of information stored there.

A couple of hundred years ago Veronica had requested a storage house be built with seventeen rooms. At the time he thought that it was quite excessive but he had never denied anything that his beloved wife had requested so he had it built. Now of course, now that he realized the volume and detail that was stored there he asked "How did you get this much stuff in only seventeen rooms?" She smiled and laid out a blue print that indicated that an additional thirty one rooms had been added over the years and she kept and cherished each and every one.

"I'm glad you finally came around to realizing the importance of our legacy." She quipped with a smile. "And we'll be adding three more rooms soon." She had that funny look on her face that she always had when she was about to unveil a secret. "Triplets?" He stood there dazed.

"No silly" she replied "Mary, granddaughter to Paul, our 365th son is having twins." He was relieved for a moment then asked "And the third one?" "Yes, well I've been meaning to ask you what you think of the name Joseph. We've never had a son named Joseph." Nicholas leaned against the wall and sighed. "Joseph" his eyes twinkled and a broad smile came across his face. "Yes, Joseph would be a good name. When?" "Oh, not for a while yet, Joann just wrote and told me about it yesterday." "Oh …" he sighed. I thought you were talking about us." "Perhaps someday: if the good Lord is willing, but not now." She replied. "In a way I'm relieved, yet, perhaps someday!" They giggled some at the thought and returned to the main house. "Now don't get any ideas." She said when he gently nudged her toward the main house.

The next several years they continued to concentrate on collecting the data and writing it all down in sequence so they figured that one day they would have a complete book. When they discussed the order by which it should be reflected they discussed several options. The most logical, it seemed was to simply follow them in chronological order but then on the other hand they gave thought to giving prominence to those who seemed to have the most impact on world affairs. Once, while discussing it the subject of Napoleon had come up. He actually was born some one hundred years before the well-known Napoleon of France and had elected to settle in the mysterious continent of Africa. He was only there for seven years before being killed by a barbaric tribe but while there he had established several colonies and was considered by many to be the father of the central continent by gathering them together into countries and setting them on the path to civilization. The world, of course knew very little about him outside of his sphere of influence yet in his own right he was revered as a patron saint of the lower central countries of Africa. Nicholas and Veronica spent many days discussing the various possibilities and yet in the end decided that although some had become more prominent than others, all were near and dear to their hearts and so the chronological sequence was selected.

One day, out of the blue they received notice that Tipper, one of their daughters who had left many years hence was coming back to stay. She informed them that although she had a good life that now God had taken her husband and her eleven children were all grown and could take care of themselves. Tipper simply wanted to return home and spend the rest of her days with her parents. They gladly accepted her back and made arrangements for her return.

Now, she was seventy eight years old and was showing every bit of it. When she finally arrived she was accompanied by three grandchildren, two boys, Jimmy and Nicholas IV, and a baby girl just barely three named Tipper Too. Of course they were excited to finally meet the famous Saint Nicholas as he was now referred to by many and He and Veronica were happy to have them there.

Jimmy, the eldest always wanted to be close to the reindeer and help. Tipper Too insisted that she was old enough to help make cookies and candy but young

Nicholas IV, even though he was not yet seven had decided that this type of life wasn't for him and he wanted to explore the unknown.

In order to avoid confusion when speaking to him he was always referred to as Nick. Since he was a strong willed child he insisted on being addressed as Nicholas IV. So more times than not, when he was in trouble they would address him very sternly as Nicholas the fourth! He liked the attention and although they didn't think of him as a bad boy they did classify him as feisty.

On one occasion he wanted to go to the storage room and was instructed that since everything in that building was very precious as it was a complete record of their history that he should not be allowed to go there by himself until he settled down and proved himself worthy of the trust. He had a bur up his butt and decided that he was old enough to visit the house on his own. He managed to obtain a lantern and proceeded to the house. Since he didn't have a key he decided that he could maybe find a window unlocked and as luck would have it he found one in the far side out of view of the others. With that he crawled into the room and started searching. He didn't know what he was looking for but he simply wanted to find out what was so precious in that building.

After searching for some time he located a room identified as Nicholas. He wondered if it was the items he was looking for and jimmied the lock to get in. Since he was Nicholas IV he considered this might be the records of his father and he wanted to know more about him. Grandma Veronica as she became known had told him at one time that after he was a little older she would show him the room dedicated to his father and mother and that at that time she would explain everything. Young Nick, of course wasn't about to wait until the grownups decided that he would be old enough to understand so he had his motivation and determined that he was going to find out in his own time.

After a bit of searching he became discouraged as many of the documents that were kept in that room were in a language that he did not understand. At one point he became so frustrated that he swung his arm across the table scattering the papers. That wasn't all that he scattered as his arm hit the lamp and sparks flew everywhere. He tried to beat out the flames as best as he could but he just wasn't able to bring it under control. Fortunately for him Barnie, one of the workers just happened to be passing by and thought it odd that even though the door was locked that there was a light inside. When he peered through the window he saw what was happening and immediately went into action. He pulled a blanket from the reindeer stable and proceeded to douse the flames. Since he had enough sense to pull the alarm he soon had a sufficient amount of help and was able to bring the situation under control. Young Nick suffered some slight burns on his hands and arms and had inhaled some smoke so he was a sick puppy for a couple of days. Barnie had suffered some severe burns on the arms and face and was out of work for several weeks. Thanks to his quick thinking though not many of the papers were lost in the fire and could be reconstructed.

"NICHLOAS THE FOURTH!" Grandma Veronica addressed the boy with a calm and stern voice. "Why is it that you think that you are not required to follow the rules of the rest of civilization? What were you thinking? Where do you get off doing what you want to do and not as your told?" You could feel the tension mount as she spoke. She stood there for a moment staring at the boy and you could see the blood boiling in her eyes. He fell to his knees drooped his head and simply responded through sobs

"I'm sorry Grandma Veronica, I really wanted to know ..." His voice trailed off. While observing him she saw the burn marks on his hands and compassion swelled within her. She swooped down and picked him up.

"It's ok, no real harm done to the contents, we can fix that. Now however we need to fix your hands. Let's see."

They returned to the main house where she and his grandma Tipper attended to his wounds. "What on earth were you thinking about?" Grandma Tipper asked.

"Why would you want to destroy all of the archives of the centuries?" "I didn't mean to" the boy sobbed "I just wanted to know ..." Once again he left the sentence unfinished.

"Well we'll just concentrate on getting you better for now and once you've recovered and had time to think on it, we'll talk again." They tucked the boy in and left the room.

"I've applied some special ointment to the burns so they won't hurt as much." Veronica told Tipper.

"Is he always that head strong?" "Not until recently" Tipper replied. He seems to be having a hard time going through a change in life as he recently lost his father."

"I know, I know" she responded "So we'll just have to do what we can to help him adjust." They peeked through the half open door and saw that he was sound asleep.

While all this was happening Tipper Too decided she could get into the kitchen not bothered by the adults and she would bake a batch of cookies. As she had been sitting there at the table for almost two weeks now and was always told that she would have to learn the basics before she could cook she watched intently while things were progressing. In her mind she was confident that she knew all there was to whipping up a batch so she started.

"Let's see!" Her mind was stepping through the process and she knew that the first step was to get everything out and place it on the table. "Eggs, milk, flower, etc., etc., etc." One thing that puzzled her though was how much of each. "Well, like Grandma Veronica always says, [we'll just have to wing it.]" Tipper Too wasn't sure exactly what it meant to wing it but she was sure she could figure it out. She got half way through her process when she remembered that the oven wasn't on. Not dissuaded she climbed up to the cabinet where the matches were and brought a couple of them down. "I'll get more just in case" she thought to herself. "That way I won't half to climb on the stove again and risk getting burnt." She remembered that her Grandma Tipper had pulled her hand back once she attempted to grab some already finished cookies off the top of the stove that were there to cool down.

When she got to the point where she needed to strike a match and set it close to the gas she discovered she had another problem. "I know they say I'm only three and can't do these things, but they forget I'll be four in a week and I know I can do this." After studying the situation for a minute she decided that she could get a long straw from the kitchen broom and attach the match. There was a roll of duct tape close by and as she had heard it so often repeated "Duct tape will fix anything." She proceeded to wrap the match to the end of the straw. "There" she smiled with confidence, "That will take care of the reach problem." So she set the oven to 300 degrees, or at least what she thought would be 300. She wasn't really good with numbers so when she saw the "5" she was confident that it was correct. After a couple of tries and a few additional straw strips she finally got the oven to respond. What happened next she wasn't prepared for. While she was manipulating the match and retyping it to the straw the gas was building up in the lower part of the oven. When she finally got the flame close to the burner it belched out a tremendous flame. Tipper Too was knocked back on her rump and sat there staring at the flames as they finally caught hold and settled down to a continuous flame. She examined herself and determined that she had not been injured so she continued. "Let's see, close the oven door so it will warm up while I finish making the cookies."

She worked at for a while and was confident that everything would be alright so she started back to the task at hand. After she whipped on the content for a while she decided that it was still too runny. The obvious solution was to add more flour. She did, and then discovered there was too much dough and it was way too dry to make a good cookie so the obvious thing was to add more milk. "Oh, Oh, no more milk! Well we'll just have to use water!" So she continued to mix and add and add and mix until she got it just right. One thing that bothered her though was that there seemed to be an awful lot of dough. "Oh well, we'll just have to wing it." She had heard that expression so often that it was second nature to her. "Yep, we'll wing it." She found the cookie cutters in the closet where she had seen Grandma Veronica take them from and started to select the various ones she liked best. "Let's see, a

Christmas tree, a gingerbread man, a ..." she spotted an area in the back of the utensil drawer that she had not noticed before.

"Wow" she thought "A pizza pan. I can make a pizza cookie. Since I've got more cookie dough than I really need I can make a real pizza cookie. She plopped a clump of her newly designed matter on to the pan and got a rolling pin.

"We'll just flatten that out for a bit, not to thin though, and we'll have a perfect cookie pizza. She continued to work at it and was getting ready to put it all in the oven when Grandma Tipper entered the room.

"What on earth is this all about?" she heard her grandma say. "Honey you'll burn the house down and yourself with it if you're not careful."

Tipper Too just stood there smiling at her grandma. She had flower all over her hair, in her eyes, on the table and spread out all over the floor.

"I did it grandma!" She said proudly. "I made the cookies for tonight."

"Honey, I know you want to be a grown up but you just have to get the basics down first."

"Oh, that" Tipper Too rolled her eyes. "I've been watching for two weeks and I know everything."

"Well first thing you'll have to do is to check your oven, it's way too hot. If you open that door the heat will burn your eye lashes off."

"I set it at 300, just like Grandma Veronica" she protested.

"No honey you set it at 500. Now we'll have to wait a half hour while it cools down.

"Good thing you came in when you did. Hu." She had a

large grin on her face. Well one thing we need to do while it's cooling down it to clean up this mess." Grandma Tipper gave her the stern eye but inwardly a butterfly twinkled and fluttered inside.

Chapter 14

"Remember in the beginning? It seems so long ago and far away. I wonder what it would be like now to go back and visit." Veronica spoke softly while she cuddled in Nicholas' arms. Always the pragmatist Nicholas replied

"What's the point? Nobody would remember you and if they did it would be stories passed down from generations past." She just smiled with that cute little smile with the tiny curl at the ends of her mouth.

"Still, sometimes I think I'd like to see the old home town."

"What?" his reply was more of a quizzical jest than then an actual question. "And get run over by those infernal noisy mechanical machines." She smiled again and replied

"Oh, they've had those for a long time now and besides they go faster, are more quiet, don't require wheat every day and they don't make a mess on the ground." She squeezed his arm and stated

"Anyway I've been thinking of going back for a little bit just to see the new things that have developed over the past couple of centuries."

"Oh, that again" he replied, "and you'd like to visit the

United States of America and see how Jennifer, Frank and the three girls are doing. Why can't they just come here? We have plenty room."

"You know why. Jennie promised Frank that the girls wouldn't be brought up in a fairy land atmosphere and we have to abide by their wishes." He huffed at that, dropped his head back on the pillow they used when sitting in the swing and mumbled something.

"What? What did you just say? Nicholas I'm ashamed of you. What if the children heard you talking like that? May be you need some soap to suck on for a while."

"Okay, okay but it's ashamed that the children are robbed of the opportunity to enjoy the benefits of the Christmas celebration just because their father is a ..." his voiced stopped in mid-sentence. Out of the corner of his eye he had spotted the two kids hiding and listening in the bush.

"Well" he spouted with a loud voice "Did you get an ear full?"

"Oh Grandpa!" Young Nicholas replied. "We were just enjoying the stars when you and Grandma came out and we didn't want to disturb you."

"And what other wolf tickets are you selling today?" Nicholas responded. "You two come on up here and sit with us a while and tell us your story."

The two children scurried out of the brush and up to the stairs. They placed themselves on the porch floor at the feet of the two grownups and Tipper Too asked them to please continue with their conversation.

"We know that things are not perfect and will never be in the world but we really enjoy listening to the stories." She continued.

"We know that it's better here but still it's fun listening to how things have developed over the years."

"Well!" Nicholas replied thoughtfully. "Perhaps we can speak to Grandma Tipper about you joining us on a tour."

Their eyes lit up and you could see the entire universe spinning in them.

"A real tour to the real world; wow that would be really keen."

"Hold on now" Veronica interjected "just what brought that on?"

"Well" Nicholas replied "You want to go on a trip, the kids want to go on a trip and I'm tired of sitting on my backside." While it was true that he was still officially in charge it was also true that Hershel, his son of just a hundred had for the last fifty years held the reigns of the operation and for the most part the two founders of this organization were put out to pasture.

No one ever doubted that Nicholas was still in charge although he had through the passing of time slowly but surely relinquished his daily chores to Hershel who had proved to be most competent in assuming the duties of the task of head master.

"Offer me one single solidarity reason why we should simply sit on the porch and wonder how things are when we have the resources to step into a new adventure and show the young ones the time of their lives." He sat there just looking at her waiting for an answer.

"Well …" She paused for a minute then stated "I don't have one single solidarity reason. Let's talk to Tipper and see if she can come up with one."

Tipper slowly pushed open the screen door where she had been listening to the conversation and said

"Well ... I" she paused "I can't think of a single solidarity reason either."

"Okay then." Nicholas looked at Veronica. His voice reflected a sense of joy that she had not seen or heard for quite a while.

"You really think this is a good idea?" Veronica quizzed with a smile on her face. "Well," he replied "It's all your fault." He squeezed her ever so gently, pulled her close to him and whispered "I'm glad you have faults."

Hershel chimed in "Well I'm glad that's settled. Now perhaps we can get on with the chores." The two looked at each other questioningly.

"Is there anybody else here listening to our private conversation?" Nicholas exclaimed.

"Dad, we've known for some time that you and mom want a change and this is the perfect opportunity to make it. This place runs like a Swiss watch. You and mom have done yourselves proud and I'm proud to call you my parents. You deserve a break today, now's the time to get away; you know the rest of the song. Take the bull by the horns and run with it."

"So be it then." Nicholas replied. "We've only one thing left to do. Honey lets go to prayer."

The following two weeks were filled with excitement while they laid out their plans for the trip. Tipper declined the offer to join them as she stated that she had seen a lot over the fifty some odd years that she spend on the real earth as it was referred to and really didn't miss it. Perhaps someday in another hundred years or so she'd want to go back but as of right now she had no desire to return. She did have some reservations about the two children as even though they were wonderful kids they were still kids. That problem was resolved when Lisa, one of the older daughters offered to chaperone the children.

"After all" she offered "I've been there once before and had a great time. All three of the children eagerly agreed to be good and follow Lisa's instructions so it was settled.

Nicholas called Hershel into his office for one last briefing.

"I've been looking for a way to accomplish this for quite some time now." He stepped up hugged his son and presented him with a piece of paper.

"It's the original deed to this part of the universe. God gave it to me with instructions to build a great nation and pass it on when the time came." His voice was choked with emotion. "Now is the time."

He gave his son another strong hug and passed the paper over to him. "It's not good bye or forever dad." Hershel objected. "Oh, mom and I will be back after our vacation but the enterprise is now officially yours. You earned it and you have assumed the responsibilities for it so," he paused briefly

"it's yours." With the ceremonies all completed and the last good byes being said they mounted the transportation vehicle and left the area.